TO SEDUCE A HIGHLAND SCOUNDREL

Heart of a Scot, Book Three
Second Edition

COLLETTE CAMERON

Blue Rose Romance®

Sweet-to-Spicy Timeless Romance®

TO SEDUCE A HIGHLAND SCOUNDREL
Heart of a Scot, Book Three
Copyright © 2021 Collette Cameron®
Cover Art: Sheri McGathy

All Rights Reserved
This book is a work of fiction. Names, characters, places, and incidents are the product of the author's imagination or are used fictitiously. Any resemblance to actual events, locales, or persons—living or dead—is coincidental.

All rights reserved under International and Pan-American Copyright Conventions. By downloading or purchasing a print copy of this book, you have been granted the *non*-exclusive, *non*-transferable right to access and read the text of this book. No part of this text may be reproduced, transmitted, downloaded, decompiled, reverse engineered, shared, or stored in or introduced into any information storage and retrieval system, in any form or by any means, whether electronic or mechanical, now known or hereinafter invented without the express written permission of the copyright owner.

Attn: Permissions Coordinator
Blue Rose Romance®
P.O. Box 167, Scappoose, OR 97056

eBook ISBN: 9781954307728
Print Book ISBN: 9781954307735

collettecameron.com

"I vow to ye, I shall keep ye safe. Ye needna fear any longer."

Dedication

For Dee – My sister in spirit!

1

Scottish Highlands
Early July 1720

Trepidation, exhilaration, and relief vied for dominance within Berget Jonston as she concealed an indelicate yawn behind her hand. Lifting the fragrant, steaming cup of milk-and-sugar laced tea to her mouth, she blew lightly as she worked her gaze over the Hare and Hog Inn's humble but cozy private parlor.

The unpainted open shutters permitted the cheery morning sun to infiltrate the dark, high-beamed chamber, which smelled slightly of smoke and last evening's supper.

Something containing cabbage and—she sniffed—

leeks, she'd vow. A half-dozen tables with mismatched chairs, a raggedy-eared red stag above the soot-stained, stone fireplace mantel, and a lopsided coat rack beside the stout arched door enhanced the rustic ambiance.

Utterly exhausted when she'd arrived last night, she'd misheard the coachman call the lodging house the Hairy Hog. Given her fanciful—sometimes naughty—imagination, that had spurred all sorts of odd visions.

Even her dreams had been invaded with images of hairy pigs with curly coats like sheep, bedchambers with straw-filled sties for beds, and breakfast plates heaped with corn mash.

She often had peculiar dreams when overly tired or troubled. She'd been both for days.

However, this establishment appeared much the same as hundreds of others across Scotland. Functional, rather than luxurious, but adequately clean and suitable for hungry and weary travelers.

After just over a week of grueling, teeth-cracking, and bone-jarring travel, the perpetual fear initially thrumming through her had dissipated to a vexing niggle. She'd ceased jumping at every sudden sound, peering anxiously out the coach windows mile after interminable mile, or fretting about the conveyance's sluggish speed.

I did it. I truly did it.

A secret, triumphant smile tipping the edges of her mouth, she sipped the delicious tea, welcoming its soothing warmth. Absently, she traced the L-shaped groove in the scarred tabletop with her index finger. At quarter-past six in the morning, only she, her sleepy—rather grumpy—companion, Mary Irving, and a savage-looking, long-haired, tartan-clad Scot occupied the chamber.

Of its own accord, her gaze traveled to where he sat gobbling his breakfast. As if sensing her perusal, he glanced up, a smile somewhere between flattered and annoyed curving his mouth.

Blinking drowsily, Mary yawned and poked at her bowl of porridge.

At a table beneath one window, the big Scot belched loudly, then chuckled devilishly—a dreadful untamed rumble—at her wide-eyed, disconcerted, and wholly critical glare. Berget's companion had speared him with several such intolerant scowls, which only seemed to amuse the man all the more.

His thickly lashed, azure eyes glinted with an unnerving combination of mischief and menace. Every now and again, his full lips twitched. Not that Berget deliberately observed him, but when he emitted unrestrained vulgar sounds…

No gentleman *ever* made bodily noises in the presence of women. Arching an eyebrow askance, Berget pointedly stared at him and awaited the expected apology.

None was forthcoming.

Instead, he patted his flat stomach with his great paw of a hand which bore a pinkish scar and, quite deliberately, burped again.

Loudly and boisterously.

A challenging grin on his whisker-stubbled face, he stuffed a kipper into his mouth. Whole. Then proceeded to chomp with hearty exuberance. Almost…aye, almost as if he *meant* to offend and dared them to call him out for his impertinence.

TO SEDUCE A HIGHLAND SCOUNDREL

What a cock-sure, Highland scoundrel.

He'd succeeded in affronting her, as he'd no doubt intended, and she presented her profile. At least he closed his mouth to chew. There was that small reprieve.

Though she'd met only a few Highlanders previously, they were reputed to be a rougher lot than Lowlanders, and even more so than the simpering English fops she encountered in Edinburgh.

Or the dandified fop she'd been forced to wed.

Lips pursed, she gave a tiny side-to-side flick of her eyes in remembered repugnance.

Lord Almighty, Manifred had been the worst sort of prancing, prissy popinjay. He'd fussed and whined more over acquiring a hangnail or freckle than any female Berget had ever met. Heaven forbid that he should acquire a spot of something on his immaculate attire or encounter a crawling creature of any sort.

Once, a snake had slithered across his path, and his high-pitched shrieks had rung in Berget's ears for days. So had his contortions and high-kneed hopping to keep from having to place his feet upon the reptile-contaminated ground.

Upon her entrance into the parlor a short while ago, the Scotsman, now so exuberantly enjoyed his meal, had examined her from her black-clad head to her toes. Evidently finding nothing of interest, he settled heavily into a chair and applied himself to his food with impressive and noisy gusto.

Unused to being dismissed so easily—for she'd never wanted for suitors, even after becoming widowed—rather than take his indifference as an insult, a little thrill of satisfaction had tunneled through Berget.

Her plan to appear ordinary and easily dismissed had worked to perfection.

Well, she was a trifle offended he could so easily disregard her, when 'twas so very hard to disregard him, poor manners aside. He was the sort of man who commanded attention. A man among men. Confident, brawny, attractive as sin, and perhaps a might arrogant too.

Such a man might've piqued more than her curiosity at one time. Before she'd married and learned the true nature of men. Before she'd sworn off the opposite sex for eternity and beyond.

A small smile teased the edges of her mouth.

She'd been wise to wear her mourning weeds from two years ago. A shapeless sack of a gown and equally hideous bonnet complete with a heavy veil covering all but her chin and mouth, unadorned and practical obsidian-colored boots, gloves, and a simple ebony cloak completed her unremarkable ensemble.

Drab as a Quaker's or a nun's attire. Nothing the least enticing or alluring unless one had a peculiar proclivity for ugly, black clothing. Collectively, her attire screamed *Leave me alone*!

And for the most part, on this tedious journey, everyone had.

To commemorate her husband's death—one couldn't very well blast trumpets, light colorful rockets, and dance with glee, no matter how overjoyed one was to be free of matrimony's encumbrance—she'd specifically chosen the items for their utter and absolute lack of appeal.

In that inconspicuous way, she'd silently rebelled.

Then, as it did now, the defiance brought great gratification.

The gown and bonnet were truly dreadful—that seamstress and milliner ought to never touch a needle again. She hadn't been able to sell them as she had most of the rest of her wardrobe as well as her jewels. Manifred had been generous in the gewgaws and trinkets he bestowed upon her, praise the saints.

Once more assuming the *faux* role of a grieving widow, she'd opted to wear the travesty on her flight to the Highlands. As she'd hoped, her attire deterred unwanted questions and unwarranted interest directed her way and also masked her identity. Today, she'd reach Killeaggian Tower, and Berget would begin her new life as a governess while Mary would be reunited with her grandmother in the nearby village of Killinkirk.

The daughter of a Scottish viscount reduced to a governess.

Giving a little mental shake, Berget admonished herself.

Nae regrets. None.

Well, she had one wee qualm. She hadn't told her best friends, Emeline LeClaire or Arieen Wallace, what she was about. However, once she was settled in her new home, she'd write them straightaway. When the danger of discovery was past.

For certain, her parents would question Emeline, who also lived in Edinburgh with her impossible aunt. Berget refused to put her friend in the awkward position of lying for her. Emeline's life was difficult enough as it was.

She bit off the corner of her toast, chewing thoughtfully. She'd known full well the irreversible consequences of her carefully conceived plan. Far better this than another forced marriage. Such a union would've destroyed her. She knew it beyond a doubt.

The fact that in the seven short weeks since the McCullough's Masquerade Ball when she'd learned of her parents' perfidy, she'd managed to secretly sell her belongings, acquire a position, arrange travel details, and hire Mary was a tribute to her cleverness as well as her parents' lack of interest in her for anything other than a means to increase their financial standing.

Left to her own devices for the most part, they'd wrongly assumed Berget would meekly comply. *Again*. It showed how little they knew their daughter. How very unlike them she was, thank the divine powers and all the saints too.

Berget's smile slipped as she considered their reactions upon discovering she'd flown.

Fury. Outrage. Retaliation.

She hadn't left a letter or other indication where she'd hied off to. Not so much as a hint. Doing so posed too great a risk of being caught, and nothing upon this earth would compel her to wed to satisfy Lord and Lady Stewart's greed and their desire to fill their perpetually empty coffers once more.

For once in their self-indulgent lives, her parents might consider economizing rather than selling their only offspring like a prize sow or heifer. Again. That they'd even suggest she enter another arranged marriage pained her beyond words.

Hadn't she sacrificed enough for them already?

They expected their only child to agree to another loveless union? To a sot even older than Manifred? To a man evil fairly radiated from?

Nae. Nae. Nae!

This was her life to live. She'd done the dutiful thing once. And had been miserable beyond words.

She pressed to fingertips to her lips, pondering. How much had the settlement been for this time?

Revulsion skittered from her neck to her hips, and she tightened her mouth.

Oh, eventually she'd forgive them—*mayhap*—but at present, fury and hurt that they'd arranged another match for her without her permission or even having the courtesy to discuss the nuptials with her made reconciliation impossible.

After many days of traveling, she was fairly certain she hadn't been followed, and they'd not be able to trace her. Not even Mary knew her real surname.

Berget was of age now. She didn't have to comply with her parents' demands. She could, and would, forge her own future, and a governess to a Highland laird's children proved far more preferable than marriage to…well, to anyone. Ever.

All her silly girlhood dreams of marriage, love, and having a family of her own had died, one by one, until the idea of exchanging vows ever again left her lightheaded and queasy. And afraid. So very afraid. A husband had absolute, undisputed control over his wife.

Her eyelids drifted shut, and her memory unwillingly flashed to four years ago to the naïve seventeen-year-old girl she been. The trusting daughter, obediently fulfilling her parents' dictates and wedding Manifred Jonston, three and twenty years her senior.

In the beginning, he'd been kind enough. As long as she kept to herself, made no demands, and permitted him to go about his life as he had prior to their nuptials.

Which meant frequenting establishments so loathsome and depraved that she nearly fainted when she'd learned of his activities. Afterward, she could scarcely stand to be in the same room with him. Her humiliation multiplied a thousand times over when she'd realized many others knew of his depravity.

Even now, bile burned the back of her throat, nearly making her retch.

In order to acquire the bulk of his inheritance, he'd been required to marry and produce an heir. After they'd wed, she'd discovered he wasn't physically capable of the latter. Or more to the point, he wasn't capable of coupling with a woman. Any woman.

A blessing that.

He'd received half of his bequest upon marriage, which he revealed when he told her she'd been sold to him for a mere five thousand pounds.

Five thousand pounds.

God, wasn't she worth more than *that*? Hot tears threatened, and she stubbornly willed them away. She did not cry in public.

She did not cry in private either.

Not anymore.

2

Most conveniently, Manifred had died of a fever. Inconveniently, a monumental scandal had arisen…

Enough.

Berget shuddered, deliberately reining in her disagreeable recollections. Nonetheless, her stomach pitched end over end, the humiliating memory quite putting her off the toast she'd been nibbling. Another sip of tea served to fortify her, however.

"Berget?" Mary gave her a queer look, disquiet creasing her brow. "Ye look unwell."

Berget would like to think her companion genuinely cared, but truth be told, likely she was more concerned there'd be any sort of delay in departing the inn.

Mary was eager to reach the village her grandmother had moved to after leaving the service of a duke as his housekeeper. Her elderly grandmother needed someone to help care for her, and as Mary reviled her position as a maid-of-all-work for a wealthy merchant in Edinburgh, she'd jumped at the chance to live with her grandmother.

"I'm fine. Just anxious to reach...um...our destination," she assured her, aware the Scot had actually stopped eating for a moment and openly eavesdropped upon their conversation.

She didn't know why she hadn't wanted him to know they were for Killeaggian Tower. It wasn't as if this was the thirteenth or fourteenth centuries and rival clans charged about razing one another's keeps or abducting the enemy's kin and ravishing them anymore.

From beneath her lashes, Berget slid him another surreptitious glance and cursed inwardly for her lack of control.

He unabashedly stared. At her.

As if he yearned to see beneath the ebony lace

concealing the upper half of her face.

She felt secure behind the delicate obsidian tatting. Nonetheless, heat blossomed across her cheeks at his boldness. Had the boor no manners whatsoever? Was this behavior what she could expect in her new home as well? She'd best prepare herself for there was no going back, she told herself firmly, jutting her chin out and squaring her shoulders.

The door swung open, and the innkeeper stepped across the threshold, wiping his hands on his wrinkled apron. He bobbed his grizzly head, his kind nut-brown gaze slightly worried. "The other passengers are already aboard the coach, Mrs. Black."

The Scot snorted and mumbled something most assuredly indecorous and most probably insulting under his breath.

Berget curled her fingers into her serviette, taking her frustration out upon the innocent cloth. Fine, she conceded. Her selection of a false name mightn't have been the cleverest, but the infuriating man stuffing his face across the room didn't know 'twas an assumed moniker. Neither did the innkeeper, though she suspected he was accustomed to being given manufactured identities.

"The driver says he's leavin' in five minutes, with or without ye," the proprietor advised.

She patted her mouth and tipped her lips upward as she placed her serviette beside her teacup. "Please inform Mr. Marshall that we'll be aboard by quarter of seven. Which, you might remind him, is the precise time he told us we were to depart. You may also tell him I expect our usual seats to be left vacant."

She'd paid extra to assure Mary would sit beside her the entire journey. Better safe and all that.

A rotund, petulant matron carrying a basket containing a hissing, yowling cat had boarded the coach yesterday and attempted to commandeer both Berget's and Mary's spots: one for puss and one for Mrs. McCurdy, who reeked of garlic and rank cheese.

Actually, the fetid odor might've been attributed to her stubby feet.

She'd ordered Mary to the conveyance's other side where the companion would've been compelled to sit between two dirty chaps. The fetid smells wafting across the short expanse for the past three days suggested neither had seen the inside of a bathtub in a goodly while.

Berget had politely, but firmly, explained to Mrs. McCurdy that she could either sit on the other side of Mary or, if she preferred, between the men herself. Given her girth, that was certain to cause the trio discomfort.

Instead, the cat, McMouser, had the dubious honor of being crammed betwixt the men. From their fierce scowls and mumbled curses, neither was happy about the arrangement. McMouser's—*ridiculous name*—incessant spitting and mewling confirmed he wasn't pleased either.

Berget was rather enjoying her newfound independence and assertiveness.

She'd also been practicing speaking the King's English rather than Scots. Her future employer had specifically asked she be able to do so, and she'd assured the registry that she could. Manifred had been British, and she'd lived in England those two miserable years before he died, so the task wasn't beyond her.

Besides, she was a Scottish viscount's daughter and had been well-schooled in refinement and decorum.

She'd almost not revealed she was widowed, but the registry office had disclosed they'd been unable to fill the position for a cultured governess for over a year and didn't think her new employer would object. They'd suggested she not make mention of the fact unless asked directly.

What difference did it make if Berget had been married, anyway?

Finding a well-bred young lady willing to live in the remote Highlands who claimed knowledge in the traditional educational subjects, and also spoke French, played the harp and lute, was skilled at archery and comportment lessons, and rode were welcome bonuses, she'd been informed.

Berget had forged her letters of recommendation and felt marvelously unrepentant for duping the registry. She wasn't quite as confident about misleading her new employer, however.

Nevertheless, she *was* qualified for the position. More so than the advertisement had required. The arrangement was mutually beneficial, she assured herself once again to silence her qualms. Her employer required a capable governess, and she'd needed to flee Edinburgh.

No one would be harmed by her subterfuge.

She was convinced she could perform the duties of the position with aplomb and skill. Why should she allow something as trivial as letters of recommendation or a dead husband to muck things up?

"We'll be along momentarily." Berget gave the innkeeper a reassuring smile, then finished her tea. She'd truly like another cup, but time wouldn't permit it.

"Aye. I'll tell him," he reluctantly agreed, veering his attention to the Scot still wolfing down his food.

Was the man hollow to each of his muscular calves? Not that she generally paid any heed to men's legs, but, encased in *cuaran* boots, she couldn't help but notice his were the size of small tree trunks.

Manifred's had been the size of twigs. *Thin*, sapling twigs.

The proprietor clasped the door handle. "Yer

mount's ready as ye requested, Graeme."

So, his name was Graeme. Given or surname?

She cocked her head. Either suited him.

The starving giant canted his head in acknowledgment while cramming a chunk of sausage in his mouth and seizing two pieces of bread in his ham-like fist. His unbound reddish-blond hair swung around his shoulders, the window-light catching the copper threaded in the wavy tresses.

"I'm near done, Barrie," he managed around his mouthful of food, earning him a disgusted noise in her throat from Mary.

While Berget couldn't help but notice his rudeness, 'twas his speech that captured her interest. He possessed one of those impossibly low, melodic voices. The kind that reverberated like muted thunder deep inside his chest. Powerful and mesmerizing and mysteriously rich. The type of voice sonnets and odes ought to be read aloud in and words of passion whispered in a lover's ear.

Dinna be a clot heid, Berget Enid Tristina Jonston.

"I'll let the driver ken. He isna goin' to be happy." The proprietor turned his regard on Berget, his troubled gaze sweeping over her attire. Pity pleated the corners of his eyes, softening his features.

How well she knew that look.

"Thank you. As I said, we'll be along shortly. His schedule won't be delayed on our account." Berget dipped her chin in dismissal, an art her mother had perfected.

This widow façade had worked well so far. She'd have to abandon it when she reached her destination, of course. No child wanted a governess who looked like an oversized raven hovering about.

Rising, Mary released an exaggerated sigh. "Thank the divine powers we'll arrive today. I dinna ken how much longer I can tolerate sharin' cramped quarters with foul-tempered felines, unwashed bodies, and uncouth louts."

She slid a sideways look at the Scot, who was in the process of wiping his mouth with the back of his hand. A grimace twisted her face and pulled her lips downward. She hadn't complained *all* of the journey—only every waking moment.

At her pointed insult, he chuckled and stood, noisily pushing his chair back. It seemed as if he did deliberately act the boor. Taller and broader of shoulder than any man of Berget's acquaintance, he possessed a confident, animal-like grace as he strode to the door. It surprised her, given his immense size and the vast quantity of food he'd consumed.

She'd expected a plodding oaf.

"Praise be to St. Christopher and St. Michael *he* willna be joinin' us," Mary muttered with a hard thrust of her round chin toward his expansive back while crossing herself.

Instinct told Berget he wouldn't willingly choose coach travel. His type preferred to be in control, atop a horse, breathing the fresh air, the wind whipping through his hair. She could almost see him bent low over his horse's back, racing across the moors, his war cry echoing harshly.

There went her imagination again.

"We'd never all fit inside. 'Tis too crowded as 'tis," her companion grumbled.

Berget stifled an impatient sigh at Mary's crossness.

Only a few more hours, and they'd part company. Still, she was grateful the girl had agreed to accompany her for a pittance if Berget covered her expenses. Doing so had reduced her already meager funds, but traveling alone was too dangerous. Even for a widow.

Suddenly, Graeme pivoted and flashed a breathtaking smile, revealing strong, white teeth. His eyes, a merry shade of blue that reminded her of summer sky, twinkled with repressed amusement.

One thick forearm clasped to his chest, he swept into an elegant bow, astonishing considering his stature, and murmured in a perfectly cultured baritone, "I wish ye *a 'coimhead gu dìomhairs* and safe travels, wherever yer destination might be."

God's speed and safe travels?

Berget went perfectly still, wariness and awareness battering her. His earlier impolite behavior wasn't easily dismissed, but even a pessimistic widow such as herself couldn't deny he was a magnificent specimen of manhood.

He possessed features too wildly rugged to be handsome, but nonetheless were striking in their architecture. A wide, high forehead, sculpted cheeks, a chiseled chin, and a granite-like square jaw portrayed a warrior's countenance.

His regard dipped to her bodice for the briefest of moments. So swiftly in fact, she wondered if she hadn't imagined the downward flick of his eyes before his focus trained on her lace-covered face once more.

To her utter astonishment and absolute consternation, her stomach flipped, and her dratted bosoms dared to perk to attention, as if to say, *Look at us again, please sir.* Never in her life had such a thing occurred. Ever. In fact, her flesh had shrunk away from Manifred's cold, thin fingers.

"Impudent Highland scoundrel," Mary muttered.

Highland scoundrel, indeed.

Holding herself immobile, Berget refused to acknowledge he'd rattled her composure. She also ordered her breasts to behave like a proper widow's should. Soft and droopy and completely unaffected.

The insolent, hard-nippled things ignored her.

He gave a wicked wink before breaking into a thick brogue once more. "Who kens, lass. Mayhap we'll meet again in the no' so verra distant future."

3

Killeaggian Tower
Later that day

In one agile movement, Graeme Kennedy swung his leg across Manannán and slid from the saddle. He arched his back, stretching his arms wide. *God' bones*, 'twas good to be home. He'd been gone over a fortnight. The third time in as many months he'd taken extended trips to either Inverness or Edinburgh on business.

He despised the city, Edinburgh in particular.

The noise, the crowds, the vermin—not all the four-legged type—and the godawful, permeating stench. He drew a deep breath into his lungs, relishing the Highland's crisp, fresh air. Soon, the heather would bloom, blanketing the hillsides and glens in lush purple hues and scenting the Highlands with sweet perfume.

There was nothing as beautiful as the Highlands in August, except for a woman's naked form. That was God's ultimate masterpiece.

"Welcome home, Laird." Robbie grinned and patted the stallion's wither. Manannán tossed his head and pranced sideways. "Shh," the boy crooned softly. "Yer lady friends missed ye."

The stallion snorted as if to say, "*Indeed. Take me to my harem at once.*"

Passing his horse's reins to Robbie, Graeme tousled the stable boy's hair. "Thank ye, lad. Brush him down well for me."

"Och, I shall." Robbie ran his hand down the horse's neck. "He's a beauty, he is."

Graeme removed his bag from behind the saddle before the boy led the stallion to the stables. Returning the many greetings directed his way, he nodded and raised a hand, his heart swelling.

Damn his eyes, but he loved this place and its people.

That was why he'd sworn to himself and to Sion as his brother lay dying, he'd strive to be the best laird he could possibly be. To make these lands productive and protect his clan, crofters, and the village until his last breath.

He needn't have stayed at the Hare and Hog's Inn last evening. Killeaggian was but a three-and-a-half-hour ride by horse, closer to seven by coach. But his meeting with Logan Rutherford, Coburn Wallace, Liam Mackay, Broden McGregor, and Bryston McPherson had lasted far into the night, and they'd all imbibed more spirits than was wise.

The others had departed before dawn, Rutherford and Wallace particularly eager to see their brides, but Graeme had lingered to break his fast.

The vision of the crow-like woman in the inn's parlor intruded upon his musings again.

Nae. No' crow.

A graceful black swan.

Her atrocious garb hid her face and figure, all but her strawberry-red mouth, delicate alabaster jawline, and a rather mutinous chin. That she was recently widowed was apparent, and her flawless manners and regal air revealed she was likely of noble birth. Young too.

An aura of mystery surrounded her, and he couldn't deny he'd wanted to see her face. To discover if the rest of her features were as arresting as those below the obsidian lace of her veil. What he could see was a complete contrast to the ugly garb she wore.

He'd also been deliberately obnoxious, simply to rile her stuffy companion who'd looked upon him as if he were offal or cow droppings. It wasn't the first nor would it be the last time he behaved in that manner. Snobbery irritated the hell out of him.

"Welcome home, Graeme," Brody, the blacksmith, called, lifting an anvil as if it were no heavier than a feather.

"'Tis good to be back," Graeme returned. "Please take a look at Manannán's left rear hoof. I think a nail may have come loose in his shoe."

"Aye. I shall. As soon as I'm done here," Brody said, slamming a piece of metal onto the anvil.

Graeme's mind ventured back to the reason he'd

been at the inn in the first place. All the Scots he'd met with shared the same concern he did: they feared another Jacobite rising was imminent.

Scotland teetered on a precipice, and an inner sense told him change was coming to this great land. Change that would forever divide her people and threaten the clans' very existence.

He loved his country, would die for her and felt helpless to stop the inevitable.

Och, he'd ponder that uncertainty later. For now, he was home, and he was hungry. He took the front stairs two at a time, grinning as he entered the keep.

He employed no butler, nor a valet for that matter. Whomever happened to be nearest the door when a knock came upon the thick wood answered the door.

His nieces called out an exuberant greeting.

"Uncle Graeme! Uncle Graeme! Ye're home!"

They ran to him, wearing identical pale-yellow frocks, their little arms outstretched, and curly hair flying about their shoulders.

"Aye, *caileagan brèagha*"—darling girls—"I am."

He scooped them into his arms and planted a kiss on their downy cheeks. Six-year-old Cora and her seven-year-old sister Elena smelled like sunshine and cinnamon and shortbread. He'd been more of a father than an uncle to them these past five years since Sion's passing.

As it always did when thinking of his older brother's senseless death, Graeme's chest tightened, the pain still rapier-sharp after all of these years. For a mighty warrior like Sion to succumb from an infected foot that had turned putrid didn't bear thinking upon. His death had thrust Graeme into the role of laird, something he'd never coveted.

It only proved how very little control any of them had upon their destinies.

What was meant to be, would be. Such was life.

Graeme knew there were whispers he ought to marry his brother's widow. Sassenach or not, Marjorie was beloved by the people, and he was fairly certain she'd be amenable to the suggestion. *Verra amendable*, he'd wager.

He, however, wasn't as certain a match between

them was wise. She'd known a husband's devotion and love. He didn't feel that way about her and was convinced he never would. Besides, his own short marriage had proved disastrous, and he'd vowed to never tread down that prickly path again.

Cora tipped her head back and grinned at him, revealing another missing front tooth. "Did ye bring me somethin'?"

"Cora," admonished her sister, though curiosity gleamed in her bright eyes as well. "Ye ken 'tis rude to ask."

Hugging them until they squealed, Graeme chuckled. "Have I ever returned without bringin' ye a token?"

The girls shook their redheads, their sky-blue eyes so like his brother's, wide with expectation.

"Let me speak to yer mother and make certain ye're deservin' of a gift." With another kiss to their cheeks, Graeme strode into the great hall, still toting a niece in each arm.

Stuffed trophies adorned one wall of the large chamber, while shields and an assortment of weaponry dating back hundreds of years were displayed on the other. A seldom-used minstrels' galley festooned with deep blue draperies occupied the area directly opposite the entry. The past two generations of Kennedys used the newer formal dining room, drawing room, and ballroom for entertaining guests.

Wearing a simple sage-green gown, the Kennedy tartan pinned in place at her left shoulder, their mother turned from speaking to a pair of serving girls. Marjorie's face broke into a wide, welcoming smile.

The kind of tender, secretive smile a woman greeting her lover gave.

Unease skittered across his shoulders.

She extended her hands and crossed to him, her long flame-colored hair, the same vibrant shade as her daughters, swishing past her shoulders. Standing on her toes, she kissed his cheek, pressing her breasts into his chest the merest bit. "Welcome home, Graeme. We've missed you."

Aye, something a good deal warmer than sisterly affection shone in her treacle-brown eyes and colored her simple greeting. He'd long suspected his resemblance to Sion accounted for her attraction to him, rather than an interest in him for himself.

She probably wasn't even aware she'd transferred her feelings. For over a year after Sion's death, she'd been a broken woman, and only the love for her daughters had kept her from sinking into complete despair.

"Thank ye." He set the girls down before crossing his arms in mock consternation. Raising a brow in a severe manner, he asked in his most serious voice, "Have my *leannan's* been good in my absence?"

"I suppose as good as a Kennedy can *ever* be," came their mother's wry reply, tempered by a fond smile as she cupped the backs of their heads.

He was almost afraid to ask what they'd been up to. Especially since they thrust out their lower lips, pointed their attentions to the floor, and shifted from barefoot to barefoot.

Where, by all the saints, were their shoes?

And more on point, what had the mischievous imps done this time?

More earthworms in the kitchen vegetable basket

because they needed a home with plenty of food? Becoming stuck in trees much too large for little lassies to climb, requiring a clan member or a tolerant uncle to rescue them? Sneaking into the library in the middle of the night to make paper dolls from *silly old books*?

He still winced when he considered the marvelous tomes that had fallen prey to their antics.

Och, the Kennedys were a brave, headstrong, and inquisitive lot, and these bonnie lasses kept everyone on their toes. Far past time they spent part of their days in the schoolroom, but finding a qualified governess willing to endure the isolation and hardships of the Highlands had proven more difficult than either he or Marjorie had anticipated.

They'd been searching for over a year now. It could be said, Marjorie was extremely selective and, thus far, the only two applicants had not met her expectations.

In the meanwhile, Cora and Elena ran free.

Graeme slipped the leather bag off his shoulder, and after rummaging about for a minute, he withdrew several colorful lengths of ribbons and new hairbrushes. "I expect ye to share the ribbons, do ye ken? Nae fightin', or I'll take them away, and there will be nae more gifts for ye."

"Aye," they chorused in unison, snatching at the thin silk strips and promptly holding them to their untamed hair. Holding hands, the girls rushed to the oversized fireplace and plopped down upon the stones before the hearth.

Despite it being July, a hearty fire blazed. A necessity in the almost two-hundred-year-old castle which seemed to suck the warmth from every room. A person's bones in winter too.

Elena sat cross-legged and set to braiding her sister's fiery curls.

Marjorie touched his forearm, an inviting, womanly smile arcing her mouth. Undoubtedly, she'd gladly warm his bed tonight, but he didn't want or need that complication.

"You spoil them, Graeme." Distinct huskiness had crept into her tone.

Uncomfortable with the direction his thoughts had

taken, he lifted a shoulder. "Canna I be a dotin' uncle?"

He withdrew his arm from her clasp on the pretense of delving in his bag again. He didn't miss her small, disappointed frown, but he didn't want to encourage her either. He could only ever love Marjorie as a sister, not in the way she wanted him to—the way she deserved to be loved again. He glanced up. "I purchased the fabric ye requested. It and the other supplies should arrive within the week."

"Did I hear my brother's voice?" A moment later, Camden, as dark as Graeme was fair but possessing the same striking blue eyes, strode into the hall. He seized Graeme in a firm embrace. "We expected ye yesterday."

"Aye, I ken." He slapped his brother's back. Since Sion's death, they'd grown even closer. "The meetin' with our neighborin' clan leaders went a wee bit longer than I anticipated."

Camden chuckled, shaking his head, a knowing look in his azure gaze. "Och, which really means ye drank too much and a warm bed was far more appealin' than the journey home in the wee mornin' hours with a fuzzy head."

"Aye." Graeme shrugged, not bothering to deny it.

A smirk kicking his mouth up, Camden rubbed his jaw. "Was it a lonely, warm bed?"

"Ye're putting yer nose in where it disna belong, little brother," Graeme said, aware of the stricken look flitting across Marjorie's face.

If Camden noticed, he concealed it.

"Are you hungry?" she asked a bit tersely, already heading toward the arched doorway leading to the kitchen.

Camden's laughter rang out once more. "When is Graeme no' hungry?"

"The same can be said of ye, Brother." Graeme elbowed him in the stomach.

Only an inch or two shorter than Graeme, Camden was just as muscled and fit and could do justice to any feast.

Grunting, he clutched his belly as if gravely wounded and stumbled about the room. "How can ye be so cruel to yer brother?" He moaned theatrically, eyes closed and shoulders hunched. "My darlin' nieces, say a prayer for yer mortally wounded *favorite* uncle."

Cora and Elena pointed and giggled at his antics.

"I am famished, but I'll take my food with me. Cold meat, bread, wine, and fruit will do. Unless Cook has Scotch pies and shortbread." Graeme adored Scotch pies, Scotch eggs, and shortbread.

"I want shortbread," Cora piped up.

Elena looked to her mother expectantly. "Me too."

"I'll have to check with Maive," Marjorie told her daughters. "I'm not sure she baked any today."

He slid a sideways glance to his brother. "If ye're available, I'd wish to inspect the crops and livestock with ye. And pay a visit to a few of the crofters. The McFees' and Millers' roofs were to have been repaired while I was away as well as the bridge over Sarnoch Burn. The fences on the north perimeter were to be repaired too."

"Aye. I can go with ye. I'll think ye'll be pleased with the progress that was made in yer absence." He winked at Marjorie. "Can ye ask for food for me as well?"

"But Graeme, you've only just returned." Disappointment shadowed her pretty face.

Likely, she'd wanted to share a repast with him and catch up. The way husbands and wives did when they'd been apart.

He wasn't sure how to tactfully discourage her romantic interest without hurting her feelings. But as time went on, it became clear that he would need to say something. The longer he waited, the more awkward the situation became between them.

Mayhap 'twas time to look for a new husband for her.

His attention fell to his giggling nieces, and his gut clenched. Och, that could very well mean the lasses would leave the keep, and he'd grown so attached to them. The thought nearly made him physically ill. But if their mother was happy...

He sighed and plowed a hand through his hair. "I ken. But the day is still fairly young, and there's always much to do after I've been gone. I promise to be home before sunset and, after a bath, I'll spend the entire evenin' with ye and the girls. We can play chess if ye like."

He probably oughtn't to have promised the game, but she was lonely, and they were the only family she had. Hers had been killed in an epidemic years ago.

She gave a reluctant nod as if aware he'd said no to more than just a meal together. "I'll only be a few minutes." She stepped through the doorway and then spun around, one hand on the frame. "I forgot to tell you," she said, her eyes shimmering with excitement. "I finally hired a governess."

He paused. "Did ye, now?"

4

Graeme couldn't help but feel she ought to have included him in the decision, even if the lasses were her daughters. "I'm surprised ye didn't wait for my return."

"I couldn't risk someone else hiring her." Defiance tinged her tone. "Her references were exceptional, as are her qualifications. I expect her next week. She's Scots, speaks French and Italian, plays the lute, is well versed in decorum, and she dances too."

A veritable saint.

The black-clad woman from this morning popped into his mind.

Marjorie spoke French, and she adored dancing.

Her enthusiasm confirmed what Graeme had long suspected.

His sister-in-law was very lonely, despite living in a keep with over sixty other people. He rubbed his chin. Aye, 'twas time to for her to wed again. But to a Scot who lived nearby, so Graeme could visit his nieces often. He'd host a week-long gathering and invite all of the neighboring clans and even the villagers for a bonfire one night.

Marjorie mustn't suspect, however. For all of her demureness, she had a temper to match her fiery hair. He'd need to be sly in implementing his plan.

She returned to the hall, a sack in her hand, and he beckoned her to his side. "Marjorie, what say ye to Killeaggian hostin' a *cèilidh* in late August?"

Her eyes lit up, a radiant smile blossoming across her face, and her earlier pensiveness dissipated. "Oh, Graeme, that would be truly wonderful. We can have music and singing and dancing. And folktales. Oh, and a feast, games, and a bonfire too."

And hopefully, we'll find ye a husband. A mon who will love yer bairns and ye.

"'Tis settled then," he said, well-pleased with his cleverness. "Ye write the invitations, and I'll have

Camden deliver them. Make a list of supplies and food ye need, and I'll see they're ordered." They hadn't hosted a gathering since Sion's death, and he expected the event would be well-attended.

She cleared her throat as she passed him his food. "Graeme?"

"Aye?" he replied distractedly, his mind already on the preparations his men would need to start straightaway. And the possible acceptable candidates to be his nieces' stepfather.

"Do I invite the Buchannans and Roxdale?" Something in her tone made him regard her keenly.

Her visage gave nothing away. However, before marrying Sion, she'd been a particular friend of Roxdale's cousin, Anna.

The Buchannans and Kennedys had never been allies, but three and thirty years ago, a rift had arisen between the families. Angus Buchannan had impregnated Graeme's Aunt Winifred, and then the sot had refused to marry her.

Graeme's grandfather abducted Angus and, with a sword at his throat, forced him to wed the lass. She died a month after giving birth to Keane, now the Duke of Roxdale. Neither clan was the least inclined to forgive the offense against their family.

When compelled to be in each other's company, the Kennedys generally ignored the Buchannans, or if forced to acknowledge the clan, addressed them with icy politesse. The reverse was true as well.

"He *is* your cousin," Marjorie offered softly. "Isn't it time to put aside your differences? You and Keane could be friends, I believe. If you'd stop blustering about like belligerent bulls."

Belligerent bulls?

Graeme was no obstinate bovine, unlike his pig-headed, inflexible cousin.

He clenched his jaw, prepared to tell her that very thing until he caught sight of Camden with his fingers poking up from his head, mimicking a bull.

His brother gave a low moo, sounding much like a demented or dying cow.

Damn him.

Sighing, he brushed a hand over his eyes. "I agree. 'Tis time to put the past behind us. Invite the lot if ye're of a mind to. I doubt they'll come, however."

She gave him a sweet, knowing smile. "We'll see."

~*~

The sun hovered low on the horizon, hues of bronze and gold and pink coloring the sky. Berget accepted a coachman's hand and stepped from the conveyance as the other groomsman set about retrieving her small trunk.

Without preamble, the brawny chap placed it on the ground with a distinct thump and, before she could utter her thanks, they bounded onto their seat and set off once more—all but deserting her.

With a silent sigh, she placed her lone hatbox and small satchel atop the chest. At once, four rough-coated grayish deerhounds loped to her side and proceeded to thoroughly smell her skirts and trunk.

"Hello," she murmured softly, permitting them to sniff the back of her hand. The quartet wagged their tails and jostled against one another to have their heads scratched.

"Aren't you handsome…" She angled her head to check their sex. Two males and two females. Um, one very pregnant female, in truth. "Er, that is, handsome laddies and bonnie lasses."

As the coach's rumbling faded away, her trepidation grew.

Not that she blamed the drivers for their haste in departing. What should have been a six or seven-hour journey had turned into more than eleven.

Another conveyance had broken a wheel, making the bridge 'twas stranded upon impassable for two hours. A certain feline relieved himself in his basket, requiring a desperate stop to air the coach and move said cat to atop the vehicle with the other luggage.

Berget was positive the ornery cat had acted out of spite.

And as bad luck would have it, one of the traveling coach's horses went lame prior to their last posting house to exchange teams.

Each unfortunate occurrence had added time to the already lengthy journey.

The delays had also put the coach behind schedule

and, with every postponement, the drivers' moods had become sullen. By the time the vehicle had rumbled into Killeaggian's courtyard—the final passenger stop on their route today—Berget was tired, sweaty, her stomach gnawed her spine from hunger, and unexpected nerves wreaked havoc with her composure.

Head tilted, she peered at the impressive castle before her. At least it wasn't quite as medieval and primitive as the employment registry in Edinburgh had indicated. It possessed neither a moat nor drawbridge.

Nor a fierce, fire-breathing dragon.

What about ghosts flitting about?

A wry chuckle escaped her. So fagged was she, she would have odd dreams tonight for certain.

How old, exactly, was the keep? How many rooms?

She counted four stories above ground, excluding the towers. Was the window to her room visible from here or did her chamber lay on one of the other sides? Would her appointed chamber even have a window?

That dark thought dampened her mood considerably.

Her bedchambers in Edinburgh and the Stewart country estate were spacious rooms decorated in her favorite colors: lavender and green. Each also possessed several windows and feminine furnishings, as well as servants to see to her every need.

A wave of homesickness engulfed her, but she stubbornly subdued it. The time for second thoughts and recriminations had long passed.

She shoved her veil off her face and over the top of her hat, blinking at the sudden light. There was no need for concealment anymore. From where she stood, eyeing the keep's four towers, arched gatehouse, battlements, and corbelling, if there were fewer than one hundred chambers, she'd forego her dinner.

No, she wouldn't. She was ravenous. Her stomach growled in affirmation.

For some reason, that thought put her in mind of the hungry Highlander this morning. He'd been a peculiar mélange of intrigue, unrefinement, and obnoxiousness. And undeniable, alluring maleness. That she'd given him a second—*or third*—thought said much of her fatigue and hunger.

She ought to have eaten more breakfast. They'd been permitted no opportunity to dine at the stopovers today. In fact, she'd barely been afforded enough time to use the necessary before climbing aboard the conveyance once more.

Truthfully, Berget was quite uncharacteristically out of sorts, rather than relieved that the journey was finally at an end. Perhaps she'd been more anxious about this initial meeting with her employer than she'd realized.

Or mayhap, a new home amongst strangers made her uneasy. Or…perchance *he'd* unnerved her this morning more than she cared to admit, even to herself.

The Highlander's brazen stare had all but undressed her.

What was worse, however, was she hadn't been disgruntled by his attentions. Being a practical sort, she attributed that nonsense to a healthy young woman's libido and feminine curiosity. After all, though she was widowed, she'd not actually lain with a man. After three fumbling, inept, and wholly mortifying attempts, Manifred had never approached her again.

Suddenly becoming aware she was the center of attention in the courtyard, Berget took account of her surroundings while pasting a pleasant expression on her face. This was to be her home. She must make a good impression, despite feeling very much the peacock in the parlor at the moment.

Several people, many wearing colorful plaids, had paused in their duties to observe her. She'd wager from their curious inspections that not many visitors—particularly of the female persuasion—arrived by hired coach and were left standing unattended, for all the world appearing to have been dumped upon the keep's doorstep much like an orphan or unwanted, flea-ridden dog.

The impressive double entry doors remained resolutely and intimidatingly closed, and she worried her lower lip. Truth be told, she'd departed Edinburgh five days earlier than she'd intended, and she wasn't expected at Killeaggian until next week. There'd been no time to post a letter in advance of her arrival.

Would her new employer be put out that she'd presumed to come earlier than arranged?

There was no help for it, however. Berget had

been forced to make a swift decision.

Her parents' revelation that they intended to announce her betrothal at the Smithertons' annual summer ball, Friday past, to none other than Sir Leslie Warrington had prompted her to move up her departure date.

A longtime acquaintance of her father, Warrington had shown an unhealthy interest in her since she was a girl of thirteen. The man's shock of white hair contrasted eerily with his raven brows and almost black eyes. He'd groped her on more than one occasion, whispering the vilest things he'd like to do to her.

He'd been most disappointed when father had betrothed her to Manifred. However, a married man himself, Warrington couldn't offer for her or object to the match. He *had* suggested another arrangement—not for the first time, she learned—but even her father wasn't foul enough to turn his daughter into a whore. Not, she believed, so much out of parental concern for her but because of society's reaction if he did.

She shuddered and rubbed her arms.

Warrington truly did make her skin crawl and

stomach churn. How his poor wife endured his attentions, Berget couldn't begin to imagine. No, she didn't want to imagine.

Three months ago, Warrington's wife had died birthing her seventh child. And now, that degenerate had determinedly and steadfastly set his sights on Berget once more. Despite the fact he should have been in full mourning still, and she'd barely been civil the times she'd been unable to avoid his company.

Disregarding her vehement protestations, her parents had moved forward with the match. More on point, her father had, and Mother—in her sweet, do-as-you're-told demeanor—had gone along with Father's arrangement.

Berget couldn't help but feel desperation hedged their insistence, and that caused her to speculate how reduced the Stewarts' circumstances truly were.

Taking a bracing breath, she squared her shoulders. Her parents' manipulation and the ugliness with Warrington was behind her. Her future was here, and she was determined to exceed her employer's expectations. She must. For she'd nowhere else to go if dismissed from this position.

Arieen Wallace might take her in, but as she lived at Lockelieth Keep, she'd have to acquire the laird's approval. Only if she found herself destitute would Berget resort asking Arieen. She loathed being an imposition.

Perusing the area once more, she offered a friendly smile to a pair of passing women. Perhaps she was supposed to use the servants' entry, but where, precisely, was that located?

Around the side? At the back?

Should she leave her trunk sitting here, practically in the middle of the drive, and go in search or simply knock on the front door? She was, after all, a viscount's daughter and not a beggar or riffraff.

She'd decided to do that very thing, but the thundering of hooves yanked her attention to the sloping, cobblestone path that ran underneath a great stone arch. Two huge ethereal figures atop equally gigantic destriers charged up the incline against the backdrop of the glorious sunset. The fading light cast them into eerie shadows, much like wild, emerging specters.

Gasping, one hand pressed to her chest, she

reflexively retreated, stumbling into her trunk and a dog or two. With a small cry, she struck the back of her calves against the chest. The blow knocked her off balance. She flailed her arms in a desperate attempt to stay upright, sadly aware she very much resembled the crow she'd likened herself to this morning.

The horsemen skidded to a stop and, as she fell, her legs in the air in a most indecorous fashion, time slowed to a crawl. Over the top of the chest she sailed, catching sight of familiar tree trunk-like calves and the grass-green background of a colorful plaid. The blue stripes, she recalled inanely, were an exact match to a pair of startling blue eyes.

The same eyes which had so boldly stared at her this morning.

Nae. Nae.

Her eyelids slid closed, just before she struck the ground hard, knocking the air from her lungs. A vise-like grip crushed her ribs, and her head, shoulders, and hips throbbed in pain as she lay there. She tried, unsuccessfully, to suck in a breath.

A dog licked her cheek, and another snuffled her neck.

What is he doin' here?

5

Of all the Scots and all the places in Scotland, *he* had to be here? Now?

The echoes of several pairs of feet running in her direction, as well as all four deerhound snouts snuffling her, infiltrated her pain and humiliation-induced haze.

Bloody, damned perfect.

What a grand entrance and wonderful impression she'd made.

Clutching at her abdomen, she tried to talk but only made weird rasping, gargling sounds, and she still couldn't draw an iota of air. Panic clawed at her, pain radiating in undulating waves from her diaphragm. The harder she tried to suck in a decent breath, the more constricted her torso felt.

"Och, dinna fash yerself, lass," the Scot said in that irritatingly wonderful voice as one of the hounds whined softly and nudged her shoulder. "Hounds, sit." he ordered firmly but gently.

At once, the dogs sank onto their haunches, their big black eyes gazing at him with adoration. Any lingering doubt that he wasn't the same man as the one she'd breakfasted with this morning dissolved the instant he spoke.

A moment later, he shoved her trunk aside. With his big, surprisingly gentle hands, he settled her skirts over her legs, his fingertips brushing her intimately in the process. A frisson of awareness sliced through her. Here she was, practically dying, and she entertained wanton feelings?

He, however, and much to her consternation, appeared completely unaffected.

Murmuring soothing, inarticulate words, he raised her to a sitting position and braced her against his oversized chest. *Hard as a brick wall chest.* "Exhale slowly through yer mouth and push yer stomach out at the same time."

Still only able to take in tiny puffs, she curled her fingers into her thighs and attempted to do as he instructed. Lord, would the unbearable pressure in her middle and lungs never cease?

People encircled them, casting more shadows over Berget and the man supporting her.

"Again. Breath in, nice and deep. Suck yer stomach in as ye do," came that deliciously velvety resonance. "Now, breathe out, and push yer stomach out."

Gradually, the cramping in her torso eased, and she was able to draw a normal breath. Well, as normal as she could with the muscled man's arms encircling her, chagrin bludgeoning her, and with a dozen or so strangers peering at her as if she were the greatest oddity they'd ever laid eyes upon.

"Thank you," she murmured when at last she managed to speak. Chin tucked, she smoothed her hands over the heavy fabric of her skirt. God Almighty. Her legs had been revealed to her thighs for all to see. She wouldn't blame her new employer for dismissing her on sight. "You may release me now, sir."

At once, he did so and then offered his hand.

Forcing herself to meet his eyes, despite the bite of mortification scorching her cheeks, she placed her fingers in his palm and was soon standing.

The dogs stood too, looking expectantly at him.

Nodding at the onlookers with a commanding angling of his square chin, he said, "As ye can see, she's all right. Ye can go about yer business again."

With soft murmurs of concern and looks of reassurance, the assembled people drifted back to whatever it was they'd been doing when she'd toppled into an undignified lump.

"Are ye indeed well?" he asked solicitously.

"Yes. Only my dignity is bruised a mite." And her shoulders and backside. Managing a semblance of a smile, she untied the ribbons to her lopsided bonnet. "I assure you, I'm not usually so maladroit."

Never, actually, before this.

She pulled the bonnet off, only to thin her lips when several large hunks of hair tumbled to her shoulders. A growl of frustration throttled up her throat.

What else could go wrong?

Sighing, she ineffectually plucked at the hopelessly crushed back of her hat. Dropping it onto the trunk, she set to work tidying her hair. She refused to meet her future pupils looking like a deranged, unkempt crow.

He bent and placed her only slightly worse-for-the-wear hatbox and satchel atop the trunk beside her lopsided bonnet. He smiled with kindness, amusement, and something warmer in his bright blue gaze. "Och, now. *Mrs. Black.* When I said we might meet again, I didna mean for ye to follow me home."

"Home?" He lived here?

Wasn't that just her rotten luck? *Oh, God.* Was *he* her employer? Once again, her thoughts flew to this morning. She hadn't been terribly pretentious, had she?

But Mary had been truly horrid. So, to be fair, had he. She allowed her eyelids to glide shut as she summoned her composure and ventured the question burning her tongue. "This is *your* home?"

She repeated herself, then could have bitten her tongue in half because she didn't sound like a poised, no-nonsense governess. No, she sounded like a befuddled clot head with cotton between her ears where a brain ought to have been.

"Aye." He swept into a gallant bow, reminiscent of his behavior at the Hare and Hog's Inn this morning. "Welcome to Killeaggian Tower, my ancestral home. I am Graeme Kennedy, Laird of Killeaggian."

And everything just became worse.

He swept his cudgel-sized forearm toward another man, greatly resembling him but possessing darker hair. "This is my brother, Camden."

Younger, though just as arrestingly handsome, Camden, an arm across his chest, dipped his square chin. A chin much like his brother's.

"Welcome to Killeaggian, Mrs. Black." His curious gaze waffled between her and his brother. "Ye've met before?"

She'd have to set them to rights about her name at once, though what explanation she could give for using a false name that wouldn't give her away, she hadn't contrived yet. Mayhap the truth would serve. A portion of it at least. Aye, that should suffice.

Before Berget could respond, the laird indicated her trunk. "Camden, would ye mind takin' Mrs. Black's luggage inside, and ask Marjorie which chamber is to be the new governess'?"

So, he knew she was the governess.

Had he known this morning too?

She couldn't conceive how that was possible.

Graeme retrieved her hatbox, tucking it under one beefy arm before seizing her satchel in his other hand.

Camden stepped forward, and Berget rescued the worse-for-wear bonnet from atop the trunk. A slight furrow pulling his hawkish eyebrows together, he peered intently between them again, and then giving a slight shrug, lifted the trunk with ease. With a sharp whistle, he signaled the deerhounds to his side. Balancing the chest on his shoulder, he marched up the steps as if carrying nothing more cumbersome than her hatbox. The great deerhounds pranced behind him.

"What are their names?" she asked to fill the awkward silence.

"Thor, Vidar, Freya, Frigg." He scratched his bristly chin. "Frigg is expecting soon."

"Viking gods and goddesses," she said slowly with a nod. "Befitting for such magnificent animals."

"I didna name them. Camden did."

Speaking of names…

"My lord, I must tell you that Mrs. Black isn't my real name." She gathered the ribbons of her bonnet and clasped them in one hand. "I wished to conceal my identity while I traveled." That had made rather a muddle of her arrival here, however. But it had been necessary to prevent being followed.

"Aye, ye *dinna* say?" Only a simpleton could've missed his sarcasm and disbelief. "Are ye really even a widow?"

He cocked a brow several shades darker than his strawberry-blond hair, his keen azure gaze raking her from shoulder to toe, then leisurely making the return journey. The hardened planes of his angular face and the disapproving downward tilt of her mouth told her he questioned everything about her.

And trusted her not at all.

This wasn't good. Was she to lose her position before even starting?

His eyes narrowed into shrewd slits. "Or...are ye runnin' away from a husband?"

"Pardon?" From his unyielding expression, she realized he was entirely serious. "I most certainly am not a runaway wife. I give you my word."

Of all the ridiculous things to be accused of.

Except...he wasn't so far off the mark. She was a runaway betrothed; a fact she had no intention of revealing.

Quite simply, when she'd decided a false name was prudent, she hadn't considered she'd have to explain her assumed identity to her new employer. What were the chances she'd encounter him prior to her arrival while using the fabricated moniker? Now, however, he believed her to be dishonest and, worse, a liar.

Within the cloak's fabric, she fisted her hands, hiding her discomfiture. How much should she tell him? He was the laird, after all, and she presumed the person who'd communicated with the registry that had hired her.

"I am a widow, my lord." No need for him to

know the circumstances or that she hadn't grieved Manifred the way a wife ought to. But then, he hadn't been the kind of husband a wife mourned either.

"Nae need to call me my laird. Nae one else does. Laird or Graeme will suffice."

Use his given name? No. Much too familiar. "Might I call you Laird Kennedy?"

"If ye wish." He hitched a massive shoulder, seemingly wholly disinterested.

A couple other less than complimentary names sprang to mind, but she pinched her lips tight. She needed this position. Berget had only been here a matter of minutes, but the phrase had already become a mantra.

Her stomach grumbled loudly, and she put two fingers between her brow where the onset of a headache niggled. The movement caused her back and bum to protest, reminding her of her humiliating tumble.

Likely, she'd be sore for several days, and no doubt sport a bruise or two as well. If only she were at home and could soak in a hot bath. She'd probably be fortunate to take a tepid hip bath weekly here.

Mayhap there was a loch nearby she could swim in, for personal cleanliness was important to her.

"I would be happy to explain everything," she said. "But might I do so inside?"

Preferably, after I've eaten, bathed, and had a good night's sleep.

She directed her attention to the people still looking on with acute interest. One could only endure so much mortification. She also prayed he would accept her explanation. The highly abbreviated version.

"Of course." His astute gaze brushed over her once more before he tipped his head, causing his shoulder-length hair to swing. Many a woman would envy the color and the soft waves. "Marjorie will be anxious to meet ye. I'm sure Camden has told her and our nieces of yer arrival."

Relief tunneled through Berget as she matched his steps. No easy task considering the length of his strides. She practically trotted to keep up with him as he marched toward the entry, not once looking to see if she kept up.

Oaf.

"Marjorie is your wife?" At least he hadn't given her notice on the spot for her deception. "I know from what the agency told me that I am to be governess to two girls, ages six and seven, I believe."

Never slowing his pace, Graeme glanced down at her, an indiscernible expression on his face. "Marjorie is my sister-in-law. My brother's widow, and yer charges are her daughters, no' mine."

"Oh. I beg your pardon. My condolences." She hadn't been aware, but then why would she? She was the hired help, not a friend or family member.

"Sion's been gone just over five years now." Graeme's voice grew gruff. "I still miss him every day, as I'm sure ye do yer husband."

There was no way Berget was scampering down that uncomfortable trail. Instead, she asked, "How did you know I was the governess?"

They'd reached the top of the time-worn stone stairs, and the doors that had been so ominously closed earlier now stood wide open. "Simple deduction. Marjorie said she hired a governess. I ken everyone livin' in this area, and ye arrived with a trunk." He gave her another one of those unnerving looks. "'Tis no' typical for a widow to seek a governess' position."

Neither was it typical to hire one.

The unasked question hung heavy and uncomfortable between them. His demeanor hadn't changed. He was still coolly polite, but she felt as if he tested her.

"That is true," she replied with forced demureness. "But I assure you, I'm qualified and capable."

"I've nae doubt that ye are," he said a trifle too casually. "Marjorie wouldna have hired ye if ye werena."

Some small satisfaction there.

"Can I assume yer late husband didna provide for yer future?" He indicated she should precede him into the castle.

"Your assumption is correct, Laird Kennedy." That wasn't a lie.

"Ye're a verra bonnie lass and still young enough to have bairns. Why dinna ye remarry rather than take a position?"

Because hell's fires would turn to ice first.

His question was far too personal for Berget's

comfort. She canted her head. "Ye're a verra braw man and young enough to father bairns. Why havena *ye* married?"

Haud yer wheesht, Berget!

A shadow swept his rugged features, and his jaw tensed for an instant. However, rather than take offense, he suddenly chuckled. "I prefer yer brogue."

He would.

"Nevertheless, I was informed that my employer prefers I speak the King's English," she said. "Or French. I also speak Italian and passable Spanish."

Odin's toes. She hadn't meant to sound boastful, but the man made her feel sorely inadequate.

A speculative gleam entered his eyes. "Och, but I'm the laird, and my word is law here. Ye'd best remember that."

As if she needed reminding.

"Do ye write and speak Gaelic?" he suddenly demanded.

He would home in on her one deficit. "Yes, but not as fluently as I'd like."

A grunt sounded in his throat. Disappointment? Disapproval? Condemnation?

Speaking Gaelic hadn't been a requirement for the position, and she almost said as much before checking her retort.

They entered the keep, and a pert little maid stepped forward and took Berget's cloak and bonnet. She offered a shy smile, which Berget returned before the maid addressed the laird. "Lady Marjorie said she'd await ye in the drawin' room."

He gave a brief nod. "Thank ye, Peigi."

So, no introduction. Because Berget wouldn't be here long enough that one was necessary?

She scarcely had a chance to take in the grand entrance, an even more impressive staircase or the mullioned windows reflecting the sun's last rays before he took her elbow and escorted her down a wide passageway, complete with suits of armor and portraits of what she assumed were various ancestors. They made several turns, and by the time he drew her before a closed door, she was thoroughly lost.

When he didn't immediately press the handle to enter, she looked up at him questioningly.

"What is yer real name?" It wasn't a question but a demand.

6

Berget started at the question. Didn't he truly know? He'd had no part in her hiring?

Clasping her hands before her, she met his gaze unflinchingly. "Berget Jonston."

"Jonston is yer married name?"

"It is."

"And yer maiden name?"

"Does it matter? I no longer use it." Stewart was a common enough Scottish name, and in her family's case, was their surname and viscountcy title. Nonetheless, she'd prefer to keep that knowledge to herself.

After a moment, he gave a disinterested shrug and made a rough sound in his throat. "Ye'll be addressed as Miss Jonston to prevent gossip since, as we've agreed, 'tis singularly unusual for a widow to be a governess."

He seemed much more concerned about that detail than she or whoever had retained her had been. She didn't object to his suggestion, however. Truthfully, she'd prefer not to be encumbered with Manifred's surname at all.

Angling her head in agreement, she dropped her gaze in what she hoped was a respectful manner and murmured, "As you wish."

This reticent business would take some practice. A great deal of practice. Diffidence didn't come naturally to her, but she bit the inside of her cheek and donned a benign countenance.

She needed this position, she repeated in her mind again for the…tenth? Twelfth time?

He stepped nearer, his size intimidating, and she couldn't help but glance upward. Good God, his chest was positively enormous. Well-muscled too, she'd vow. Could she even wrap her arms around him?

She'd like to try.

That realization sent heat pooling to her middle.

Laird Graeme Kennedy was twice the breadth of Manifred. She'd wager all the tartans in Scotland he had no trouble bedding a woman and neither had he a propensity for young boys as her husband had.

The laird smelled of horse and sweat and outdoors. A muscle ticked in his jaw as he bent his neck until his face was but inches from hers. So close she could see the rough stubble of his beard and the silver flecks in his icy blue eyes.

"Just so ye ken, *Miss* Jonston, I'm no' found of subterfuge. I'd send ye on yer way—"

"Because I traveled under an assumed name?" Berget interrupted. He knew nothing of her situation, yet he would judge her dishonest for protecting herself? "Do you truly believe I'd journey to this..." she waved a hand in the air, "isolated location if I had nefarious intentions? Whyever would I do that?"

Ye did forge yer recommendations, a nasty little voice reminded her.

The coldness in his unrelenting gaze told her that taking on an assumed identity *was* reason enough to distrust her. What an arrogant, self-righteous, judgmental—

Stop!

Counting to five, she drew in a calming breath.

She must convince him otherwise.

He didn't know her circumstances, and he was simply being cautious. "I'm not without integrity, Laird Kennedy, and I am trustworthy." Neither was she a saint with a glowing halo. "When I applied for the position, I told the employment registry that I was widowed, well-educated, and that I carry noble blood in my lineage."

That caught his attention. "And yet ye accepted a governess' position *in this isolated location*?"

Oh, how she wanted to tell him to bugger himself.

Instead, she tried reasoning with him. "I'm sure you're aware that many aristocratic families have empty coffers and with dowerless daughters..."

"I dinna care about yer lineage or that ye've been widowed. Neither do I care what reasons prompted ye to apply for and accept the position as governess." He brazenly touched one of her curls, his voice silky soft yet fringed with menace. "What I do care about, Miss Jonston, above all else, is my family. And my instinct tells me ye're no' bein' completely forthright. I promise ye, I shall have yer whole tale eventually, and then I'll make a decision about whether ye stay or no'."

"I..." Berget swallowed, but refused to avert her gaze. To do so would make her appear guilty. She *was* guilty of forgery and of running away from an unwanted marriage. The former scraped away at her conscience.

The little silver flecks in his eyes glittered, mesmerizing her as they stared at one another, the silence growing tenser and more sensually charged with each passing moment. How could she possibly be sexually attracted to him? She could scarcely abide him.

Her disloyal body proclaimed otherwise.

"What? Nothin' to say now? Nae words of protest? Nae feeble excuses?" he softly taunted, his nostrils flaring as if he inhaled her scent as she had his.

What could she say to prove herself?

They were strangers, after all.

A chill scuttled from her waist to her shoulders,

and she barely suppressed a shudder. She wrestled her dread under control. She couldn't succumb to his intimidation or her own guilt.

The door swung open to reveal a stunning redhead, and she nearly wept in relief. At once, the woman smiled and pressed Berget's gloved hand between both of her palms.

"Berget, I'm so pleased you are here. I've eagerly been anticipating your arrival. I am Lady Marjorie Kennedy. You must call me Lady Marjorie and, naturally, I shall call you Berget. We don't stand on formality here, unlike the Lowlands or England. Do we, Graeme?"

"I'd prefer she be addressed as Miss Jonston, Marjorie," the laird said in a tone that brooked no argument.

Sending him an adoring glance, she sighed. "Must we?"

Ah, so that was which way the wind blew. Good to know.

If he noticed his sister-in-law's worshipful demeanor, he didn't respond in kind. That might also prove a useful snippet to store in the recesses of Berget's mind.

"Aye, especially as ye want the girls to learn proper comportment." He gave Berget a look that suggested he doubted she knew which spoon or fork to use, let alone the intricacies of social strictures.

Should she tell him how utterly boorish *he* was being?

Somehow, she didn't think he'd give a ragman's scorn. His behavior this morning at the inn certainly confirmed that. He was an absolute hypocrite for finding her wanting when he'd been a...*pig*.

"Excellent point," Lady Kennedy conceded, succeeding in returning Berget's wayward musings to the present.

Berget curtsied. "Lady Kennedy. Thank you for this opportunity. I trust I shall not disappoint."

"Lady Marjorie," her ladyship gently corrected. "*Je prévois tellement de faire connaissance.*"

"*C'est un privilège d'être ici.*" It *was* a privilege to be here, and Berget looked forward to becoming acquainted with Lady Marjorie too.

The laird's forehead crumpled as if he was annoyed they'd spoken in French. Good. She'd be sure to do so at every opportunity, if only to be an irritating sliver in his finger.

The lovely Englishwoman ushered her inside the tastefully decorated room. 'Twas such a contrast to the rest of the keep, Berget couldn't help but gape. So different was this chamber, it seemed as if she'd stepped into a different world; this one rich and cultured and the other untamed and primal.

Which was its laird?

Need she even ask?

She cut him a covert glance to find him peering at her, his features unreadable.

At Berget's expression, Lady Marjorie laughed and swept a hand before her. "This room, a ballroom, and a few others were added to Killeaggian four decades ago. I redecorated them when I first came to live here as a bride almost nine years ago." Her countenance grew melancholy, sorrow filling her kind, dark brown eyes. "Sion helped select the furnishings."

She'd loved her husband. Very much if she yet grieved him.

Compassion washed over Berget, and not a little guilt that she'd spared Manifred no such emotion. To be fair, he hadn't spared her any consideration either.

Even now, the shame of his unnatural preferences made hot bile rise in her throat. When she'd told her parents and begged to be permitted to move back home, they'd refused her request, claiming every marriage had trials to overcome.

Trials?

God above, he'd been a debaucher of young boys. And her parents dismissed it as casually as if he'd used the wrong spoon for his pudding.

Resentment yet simmered toward them that they condoned the match, for surely they must've suspected his perversity. They'd also refused her request to live with them after Manifred's death until the scandal.

Within a month of Berget becoming a widow, an appalling journal had been stolen that listed the names of the patrons who frequented a certain despicable residence in Edinburgh. Somehow, the journal made its way into King George's presence.

Perhaps in an effort to counter his unpopularity,

the king saw fit to imprison or hang several of the guilty parties and, in multiple cases, seized their properties and funds. Manifred's name had been amongst those exposed for his *blasphemous sins*.

Fear of the king's wrath prompted Lord and Lady Stewart to vow they'd no knowledge of Manifred's deviant behavior and to welcome their poor, misused daughter back into the family's bosom.

Graeme Kennedy had followed her and Lady Marjorie inside, but rather than plant his large form on one of the sofas or chairs, he rested his shoulder against the fireplace mantel and regarded Berget.

Not unkindly, but with a definite air of suspicion.

Belatedly, she realized she'd never curtsied to him.

Had he taken it as an insult?

Or proof that she lacked the essentials to educate his nieces in social etiquette? Mayhap that's why he'd looked askance at her. He did outrank her but, in fairness, she'd been winded and unsteady on her feet in the courtyard.

She'd certainly started off on the wrong foot with

him. And while her ladyship might've retained Berget, as laird, he held the power and the purse and would dismiss her in a blink. Not a doubt lingered that he meant what he said about his family, and the way he studied her made it abundantly clear he didn't trust her.

Where had the mocking, mirthful man of this morning gone to? Or the kind, considerate Scot who'd assisted her in the courtyard? The man lurking beside the fireplace was frightening in his intensity. Part of her admired his strength and his desire to protect his family, even as another part wished she hadn't used a contrived name.

And risk being followed?

Nae.

Warrington wouldn't give up easily. Neither would her parents.

She knew that absolute truth in her innermost being.

No, she'd done what she must for self-preservation. Perhaps someday, she'd be able to reveal the entire truth to the laird and to Lady Marjorie. When they'd come to know and trust her and wouldn't be appalled. When she'd proved herself and didn't fear immediate dismissal.

Berget cut Laird Kennedy a side-eyed glance.

His gaze probing and intrusive, he'd folded his arms and crossed his ankles.

Fighting the overwhelming urge to swallow, she dropped her attention to her clasped hands. She would not be ashamed before him, but she must be polite and deferential. The latter proved the more challenging for a woman born to a high station. Nevertheless, she was prepared to do precisely that. The requirement came with the position.

A commotion echoed outside the door before it swung open. Two adorable little redheaded girls in matching white nightgowns, bare pink toes peeking from beneath the hems, and clutching their Uncle Camden's hands timidly ventured inside. Blue eyes round—*their uncles' eyes*—they turned uncertain glances on Berget.

A doll cradled to her chest, a hint of mischief twinkled in the younger girl's eyes, while serene intelligence shone in her sister's.

Berget adored them on sight.

She sank into a low curtsy that would've impressed the king himself. She intended to show these people she could act the perfect lady and hopefully win their favor. "Miss Cora. Miss Elena. Sir."

"*Sir*? Did ye hear that, Graeme? I'm a *sir*." Chest puffed out in an exaggerated fashion, Camden gloated. "I've been tellin' ye I deserve more respect." Chuckling, he winked naughtily at her as he ushered his nieces further into the room.

Despite her effort to appear unaffected and professional, her lips quivered. Camden was a charming rogue. So had his brother been this morning. Graeme had also been an ill-mannered barbarian, belching and chomping his food, and he now acted the arrogant, affronted oaf.

"Before yer head swells with inflated self-importance, consider the source, Cam," Graeme drawled.

Berget flinched as if struck, his arrow striking home as he'd intended.

What, precisely, did he mean by that slur? Using a

false name wasn't such a horrid deceit that she deserved to be so ill-treated. Something more went on here, she'd vow.

Camden exchanged a glance with his brother and shied a sable brow upward questioningly.

The merest crimping of Lady Marjorie's coffee-brown eyes indicated she'd noticed the slight directed toward Berget as well. "Graeme..." she chided softly.

But when he, too, slanted a brow up in umbrage, she didn't finish.

The younger girl—*Cora?*—played with a tight curl by her ear. "She's no' auld and ugly," she whispered loudly to her sister.

"I told ye she wasna when I saw her through our chamber window," the older girl, Elena, said sagely.

Cora adjusted her doll under her arm, leaned forward, and squinted. "I think she has all of her teeth too, and..." She sniffed deeply. "She disna smell foul. And she has pretty eyes. They're the color of heather." Head angled, she demanded, "Do ye fart and belch or pick yer teeth?"

Nae, but yer uncle does.

7

Before Berget could respond Camden laughed, and Lady Marjorie's face crumpled into a mortified grimace.

Berget mulishly refused to so much as dart a brief glance in the laird's direction.

Suddenly, panic filled Cora's face, and she shrank against Camden. "But why is she dressed like a crone? Mama, is she a *ban druidh*?"

Her sister's face paled too, and she edged nearer her uncle.

"Cora," her mother admonished gently. "You're being disrespectful to Miss Jonston. Do you think so little of your mama as to believe I'd hire a witch to instruct my darling girls?"

Berget summoned her most comforting smile and

held her skirts out. "They are hideous, aren't they? I wore this so I wouldn't soil my other gowns while I traveled. Black hides the dirt much better." She thought, perhaps, the laird snorted or grunted, but she refused to look his way. "If you'd like, and with your mother's permission, I can tell you a fairytale tonight. That way we can become better acquainted."

It seems she might have to wait longer to fill her hollow stomach, but if the delay earned a degree of trust from her charges, it would be worth it.

The girls looked uncertainly at their mother and uncles in turn.

Straightening, Laird Kennedy gave the girls a warm smile. "I'll be there too, lasses."

His gaze snared Berget's.

Yes, distinct suspicion crinkled his expressive eyes, the color of the sky after a thunderstorm blew by.

"I'd like to hear what sort of *fanciful* stories Miss Jonston recites," he said.

His double entendre didn't escape her, but she fixed a polished smile on her face. She needed this position, she reminded herself again for the umpteenth time. So much easier to remember that critical fact when the infuriating, beastly Laird Graeme Kennedy wasn't nearby being, well...*beastly*.

Camden leveled his brother an inquisitive look. "She nae be a witch, lasses. She has lovely skin. Nae warts or moles, and banshees and *ban druidhs* dinna have eyes of the color of amethysts."

Unmistakable admiration resonated in his voice as well as the gaze he turned upon her.

Dual paths of heat flamed up her cheeks, though she offered a small, grateful smile.

That was a complication she hadn't foreseen or needed. To cover her discomfit, she summoned what she hoped was a poised smile for the girls. "I think you'll like one of my favorites stories from when I was a little girl: *Cendrillon*. 'Tis the story of a sweet serving girl and a handsome prince. They fall in love but face many challenges."

Another rude noise echoed from the vicinity of Laird Kennedy, but she doggedly kept her focus on her new charges. The more time she spent in his company, the less she liked the obnoxious man.

"Graeme, can I fetch ye a drink of water for whatever ye have stuck in yer throat?" Camden mocked.

Ah, he'd heard his brother's grunts too and took them for what they were. Disapproval.

With each passing moment, Berget liked Camden more and more.

"I love stories," Cora said, bouncing on her toes.

"Perfect. I enjoyed that tale very much as a child myself," Lady Marjorie agreed, taking her daughters' hands. "Miss Jonston, if you'll come with me, I'll show you your bedchamber on the way to the nursery. 'Tis but two doors down. Oh, and Graeme, your bath is prepared for you. Shall I have a tray sent up?"

"Nae. I'll come to the hall after I've bid the wee ones goodnight."

Did Lady Marjorie regularly order her brother-in-law's bath drawn? Perhaps that was a typical duty of the lady of this keep. For certain, Mother never ensured Father's bathwater was prepared. But things were done differently in the Highlands.

What *other* domestic duties did Lady Marjorie

perform for him?

At once, Berget squelched the uncharitable thought. 'Twas none of her business what the relationship was between her employers.

At the threshold, Elena paused. "Uncle Graeme? Are no' ye comin' too?"

Clearly, the girls were very close to their uncles, especially the laird.

"I'll be along soon, *leannan*," he said, fondness in his tone and gaze. He exchanged a private look with his brother, which raised the hairs on Berget's nape. "I wish to speak with Camden first and then have my bath. I promise I'll say goodnight before I sup."

Nary a word had been said to her about a bath or food, both of which sounded heavenly.

She closed the door behind her, but the latch didn't quite catch. The door drifted open an inch. With a hasty glance to Lady Marjorie, several feet farther along the corridor, Berget leaned in to pull the panel shut.

"Dinna let Berget Jonston's pretty face turn yer head, Brother."

Berget winced at the aggression in Laird Kennedy's warning.

"Why, *Brother*, do I detect a wee smatterin' of possessiveness in yer voice?" Sarcasm heavily weighted Camden's response. "I saw the way ye looked at her."

"Dinna be an imbecile. She's a damned governess," Laird Kennedy snapped.

And too far beneath his notice?

Resentment and humiliation battled for supremacy, but she firmly quashed both.

Camden only grunted at his brother's fierce declaration.

"I need ye to go to Edinburgh on the morrow, Camden. I dinna think she's who she claims she is, and I believe she's guardin' a secret."

Oh, God.

~*~

Graeme took the fastest, though not the coldest, bath of his entire life after explaining to Camden what he needed him to do. Pouring a pitcher of tepid water over his head, he washed the lather from his hair. In his haste, soap ran into his eyes. Blinking against the burning sting, he reached out blindly for the towel atop the chair beside the tub.

Once he'd dried his face, he scrubbed a hand over his jaw. No, he wouldn't take the time to shave. He rose, swiftly toweled off, and dressed.

This very minute, Berget was with his nieces, and though he didn't believe she would harm them, she was correct to think he didn't trust her. She was concealing something. Her lavender-colored eyes gave her away.

Graeme had an instinct for such things, and since he'd met her in the inn's parlor this morning, that same intuition had been on high alert. Mrs. Berget Jonston wasn't what she seemed, or who she said she was. He'd wager all the whisky in Scotland she had a secret she didn't want known. Or she was hiding from someone.

The what and who made all the difference whether she stayed or he dismissed her and bundled her aboard the next coach to Edinburgh.

However, she'd promised to explain everything,

and he wouldn't permit her to seek her bed until he had the truth from her. He doubted she'd be completely forthright, but he'd have whatever her version of the truth might be.

At first light, Camden would leave for Edinburgh and do what he did best. If there was a secret to be uncovered or a mystery to be solved, he was the person to unravel the details.

Graeme hadn't a doubt that when his brother returned, he'd know every aspect of Berget Jonston's life down to her favorite color and foods she disliked. And, most importantly, why she'd fled to the Highlands.

Actually, he planned on knowing that particular detail before Camden returned. Harboring her might portend a threat, and he wanted to know exactly what to expect.

In the meanwhile, he'd assure that she was supervised at all times. When she wasn't actively instructing the girls, she could help Marjorie prepare for the upcoming gathering. He'd keep Berget Jonston so busy with one task or another, she'd have no time for anything untoward.

As he fastened his belt around his waist, he pondered again; what had possessed a young, beautiful, and obviously gentle-bred widow to accept a position as a governess in the Highlands?

He made a scoffing sound deep in his throat.

If she was truly a widow. Surely, she'd had other marriage offers.

He wouldn't lie to himself and deny he hadn't found her damned bewitching. In the courtyard, as he held her against his chest and she'd struggled to breathe, her light fragrance had teased his nostrils.

Lemon and sunshine and her own warm, womanly scent.

When he'd bent near to fondle her silky russet curl, though she didn't flinch away, distinct leeriness shadowed her unusual amethyst eyes. There was a desperation about her too, and that was what concerned him more than anything.

He knew full well what desperation could drive a person to do. He'd seen his fellow Scots during the Jacobite rising resort to measures he'd never have believed them capable of.

Even so, the English brutality had been far worse.

Less than an hour after his nieces had left the drawing room, Graeme strode to Cora and Elena's bedchamber. Every night that he was home, he tucked them in, something he'd promised Sion he'd do.

After a few minutes of his nieces riding around on his back as he pretended to be a horse or a lion or whatever animal they'd decided he was for the evening, or a bout of tickling until they shrieked for him to stop, the girls said their prayers and scrambled into bed, giggling and begging to stay up for a bit longer.

Usually, Marjorie was present as well. After they'd kissed her daughters, he'd draw the bed curtains, except for a crack to allow the firelight in to alleviate any fears of the dark. Then he and Marjorie would bid each other a polite goodnight and go their separate ways for the evening.

Tipping his face toward the ceiling, he stifled a groan. *Beef wit.*

He'd invited her to play chess tonight. Mayhap she'd forgotten.

Of late, she'd been more and more reluctant to part company after the girls were abed, and he'd contemplated finding excuses to keep from bidding the lasses goodnight. But his infernal honor wouldn't permit it.

He'd made a vow to Sion, and he was a man of his word.

Graeme's carrying out his promises to his brother had only fueled Marjorie's infatuation by forcing him into a parental role. Not that he minded, for he adored the girls. But the time had come to distance himself a mite.

He entered their bedchamber and glanced around.

Except for the hearty fire's hissing and crackling, silence greeted him. Stepping further into the room, he frowned. Of Rona, the girls' nursemaid, there was no sign, and neither was Marjorie with her daughters.

Hands on his hips, he scowled.

Berget Jonston wasn't attending her charges either. She'd wasted no time deserting her post, and he was even less impressed than he'd been earlier.

To be fair, he'd taken longer with Camden than he'd anticipated, but she knew he was to join them. She ought to have waited.

Scraping a hand through his still damp, shoulder-length hair, displeasure turned his mouth down as he methodically examined the cozy chamber. A three-pronged candelabra glowed on a nightstand beside the canopied bed the girls shared. The curtains had been drawn across the foot, but the sides remained open.

Shite. Anger thrummed through him.

How could Miss Jonston have been so careless as to leave tapers burning and also the bed curtains undrawn? By dawn, the chamber would be freezing.

Had the woman no common sense?

Another mark against her. Mayhap he wouldn't wait for Camden's return to send the pretty but useless piece of baggage on her way.

Stifling another curse, lest he wake his sleeping nieces, he strode across the chamber. What met his infuriated gaze stopped him in his tracks.

A lass cradled on either side, Berget Jonston lay fast asleep. In repose, her wariness and reserve absent, she looked even more stunning and innocent. Not at all like a villainess or conniving wench.

Her eyelids flickered. Did she dream?

8

Unabashedly, Graeme looked his fill, noting the hollows beneath her delicate cheekbones, her slightly parted bowed mouth, and the fine arc of her winged brows. No one could mistake her for anything but what she was: a noblewoman.

What was her story? The real story?

He itched to know. Och, he itched for more than that.

He didn't know whether to be alarmed or delighted that Cora and Elena had accepted her so quickly. That said much of her character, for although the lasses weren't particularly shy, neither did they take to strangers readily.

Come to think of it, the deerhounds hadn't so much as barked at her in the courtyard. By nature, the dogs were gentle creatures, but they'd been trained to be guardians as well as hunters.

Hands on his hips, he tilted his head.

Where the devil were Marjorie and Rona?

Graeme bent and gently shook Berget's shoulder. She murmured something unintelligible but didn't awaken. A wave of compassion swept over him. Likely, she was utterly exhausted. Nevertheless, she couldn't remain here, and he would have his promised conversation with her.

"Miss Jonston." He nudged her harder, and the arcs of her thick eyelashes fluttered, gradually lifting.

"Hmm?" Yet in a sleep-induced fog, she stared at him blankly. She blinked, a tiny smile quirking her mouth, before she became fully awake. Her eyes flew wide, and her mouth dropped open in shocked embarrassment.

A low chuckle escaped him.

She sent him a quelling look before schooling her features into passivity. "Can you move Cora, please, so I might rise?"

With a brusque nod, he swept his slumbering

niece into his arms, enabling Berget to slip off the bed. He didn't miss her stiff movements or the slight wince as she righted her appearance.

From her journey or her fall?

She'd insisted she wasn't hurt, but from her measured movements, he'd forfeit all the haggis in Scotland her backside bore bruises.

He slid Cora beneath the bedcovers, then drew the curtains.

Taking a cue from him, Berget pulled the curtains nearest the fireplace closed.

"Leave a crack for light," Graeme whispered.

She cast him a swift look, then darted her gaze to the fire before nodding.

She was astute. He'd give her credit for that if naught much else.

He blew out the tapers in the candelabra and jutted his chin toward the door, indicating she should precede him.

Once in the corridor, she stoically turned to face him. She had pluck.

He admired courage in anyone.

Even in the muted light, he detected her rosy cheeks.

To her credit, she met his gaze directly. "I beg your pardon. After the story, the girls asked me to stay until they fell asleep. I must've dozed off. I assure you, it won't happen again."

His earlier anger had evaporated. He still couldn't explain the lasses' reaction to her. Or the dogs' either.

"I ken ye're tired, but I would have a word with ye, Miss Jonston."

"Of course." Berget practically swayed on her feet from exhaustion, but he'd already discerned she was a prideful woman despite her humble circumstances. He'd vow she'd topple over before admitting how sore and spent she was.

Another, more insidious, thought intruded.

Or…was she so desperate for this position that she was afraid to refuse him?

Had she been offered food? A bath?

She had better have been. The Kennedys were known far and wide for their hospitality.

Taking her elbow, he guided her the few steps to

her room. "Where's Marjorie?"

"She said she had a special meal prepared for your homecoming and wanted to see to the final details."

And she'd left her daughters in a stranger's care. That alarmed him and also alerted him that he couldn't wait until the gathering in August to speak to his sister-in-law.

"And Rona?"

"Lady Marjorie sent her to the kitchen to ask for a tray for me." They'd arrived at her bedchamber door. She gazed at him solemnly. "The food is likely within."

Rona had probably already sought her bed in the servant's chamber attached to his nieces' room. Those vixens awoke before the sun did and ran the girl ragged. No doubt the nursemaid was thrilled a governess had been hired.

He opened Berget's door and stood aside for her to enter.

After hesitating, she lowered her head and swept inside.

No bath awaited her, but a food tray sat atop the

table near the window. He'd order her a bath after they spoke and make certain the oversight didn't happen again.

Graeme followed her into the room, taking care to leave the door wide open. While many lairds dallied with their servants, he wasn't among them. He felt it an abuse of power, for no lass valuing her position would dare say no to her laird's demands.

He'd had more than a few lovers over the years, willing widows and the like. But never once had he tupped a servant in his household. And he always took care not to father any bairns.

The candle's glow cast soft shadows on Berget's face. She truly did have lovely skin. Alabaster smooth and creamy. He curled his fingers against the impulse to trail them over the pearly expanse.

She looked longingly at the food, but with fortitude he couldn't help but admire she turned her attention to him. "You wished to speak with me?"

"When did ye last eat?"

Her brows shied high on her forehead, and she swallowed. "'Tis of no import."

He stepped nearer, and her violet eyes grew wide and slightly alarmed, but she didn't retreat.

"I asked ye a question and, as laird, I expect an answer, lass."

A spark of indignation flared in her eyes, but she tamed it just as quickly.

"This morning at the inn."

Christ. No wonder she looked about to collapse.

"Sit. Eat."

He pointed to the chair, and she obeyed at once.

Not out of respect for him, he suspected, but due to her growling stomach's demands. And quite possibly, fear she'd lose her position. He didn't like how that made him feel. No female ever had reason to be afraid of him before.

A gasp of delight escaped her when she lifted the cloth covering the food. Cold meats and cheeses, bread, fruit, oatcakes, Scotch pies, and shortbread met her perusal. A bottle of wine also stood nearby. "I cannot possibly eat all of this."

"I'll join ye." Graeme patted his torso as he pulled out the other chair and sat. "I'm famished too. We can talk while we eat if ye dinna object."

As if she would.

"But what about your dinner with—"

"I said I'd be joinin' ye, Miss Jonston." He'd deal with Marjorie later. This might be just the thing to send a strong message to his sister-in-law. Cocking a warning brow, he leaned forward, elbows on the table.

Berget's reluctance had been almost indecipherable. She dropped her gaze deferentially. "As you wish, Laird Kennedy."

He checked a grin. Her way of letting him know she didn't want to comply but would, because he was the laird. Normally, that would satisfy him. He expected obedience—was accustomed to it.

"There's only one glass for the wine," she said, lifting the hand-etched goblet an inch.

He winked and filled the glass. "I dinna mind drinkin' from the bottle."

A slow arc curved her mouth, and Graeme nearly spilled the wine with the exquisite transformation her smile induced.

"I truly cannot figure you out," she said before

taking a dainty bite of cheese. "You're quite an enigma."

No servant would dare be so impudent, but he was fast learning Berget Jonston was no ordinary woman. And truthfully, he rather liked her frank speech.

"I might say the same of ye." A piece of bread in his hand, he motioned toward her. "Why are ye really here?"

At once, reservation swept across her features, and she pointed her gaze to the apple slice she held. "Because I needed a position."

"Why? I'm nae fool. Nobility disna seek employment. Ye must have another reason, and as ye'll be in charge of the care of my nieces, I'll have it from ye." He slung an ankle over his knee. "How long have ye been widowed?"

The last wasn't any of his damned business.

She stiffened before slowly bringing her eyes to meet his. Her lavender gaze probed his, almost as if she sought to see into his soul. It stirred and unnerved him more than he cared to admit. It also sent his blood humming through his veins in sensual awareness.

His attraction to her had been immediate and powerful. Even at the inn, her siren's call had beckoned Graeme. Her allure rattled and enticed him, a juxtaposition of temptation and discomfort that threatened his self-control.

That he could neither afford nor allow.

"Lass? I'm waitin'." His words rang harsher than he intended.

Wariness crept across her features. She inhaled, her chest rising as she filled her lungs, and she set aside the piece of chicken she'd been nibbling. "My laird—"

"Graeme," he corrected, refusing to examine why he insisted she address him by his given name.

Hands folded primly on the lap of her hideous gown, she said, "I was widowed two years ago after a two-year marriage."

"Ye were married verra young." He uncrossed his leg, not liking the way his gut clenched to think she'd been wed so young. It wasn't uncommon, but he'd drive his blade through any man who looked at his nieces and his daughters if he had any before they were at least eighteen.

A sad half-smile bent her pretty mouth. "At seventeen."

"Were ye happy?" He pushed the mark with the question. But he'd know as much about this woman as he could. The more she volunteered on her own, the more he believed he might trust her.

"No. 'Twas an arranged marriage. He was much older than I." Tension sharpened her features, and something in her tone tangled the knot in his middle further.

"And?" He lifted the bottle to his lips, wishing it was whisky. This woman discomposed him as no other ever had. Especially after but a few hours' acquaintance. He told himself his acute interest was simply because she was a stranger and was to live under his roof.

Bloody liar.

Throwing her serviette atop the table, she leveled him a frustrated glare. "Why must you interrogate me? I swear, I've committed no crimes. As I've said before, I am qualified for the position. I *need* this position."

Fear and desperation made her voice husky.

His determination wavered in the face of her obvious upset. But he couldn't safeguard his clan, family, nieces, or her if he didn't have the whole of it. *Safeguard her?* Aye. For all of her bravado, everything in him shouted she needed his protection too.

"Still, I would have yer answer, lass."

"I fear you'll dismiss me," she admitted, her voice the merest sliver of anguished sound. A single tear tracked down her right cheek.

Recriminations buffeted Graeme, but he stifled the emotion.

He was the laird.

He had a duty to guard against any type of trouble, no matter if it came in the form of a beautiful, doe-eyed young woman with the most kissable mouth he'd ever laid eyes upon. History was rife with men taken in and deceived by women. Samson and Delilah immediately sprang to mind.

"I canna promise no' to, Berget, but I can promise I shall if ye dinna tell me the truth. All of it."

Eyes luminous with unshed tears, her mouth slightly parted, she wrapped her arms around her middle in a self-protective gesture. She swallowed, the graceful column of her swan-like throat working.

"Manifred," she spoke so softly, he had to strain to hear her.

He bent nearer her across the table.

She raised her gaze, wounded and leery, for a flash, then dropped it to her hands clamped together in her lap. "He was my husband. He had an unnatural preference for...boys."

"Christ on Sunday," Graeme swore, gall stinging his throat at the thought of an innocent subjected to marriage with a molly and a sod.

Rosy color bloomed across her cheeks, and she closed her eyes for a blink, as if uttering the loathsome words aloud was more than she could bear.

That she would reveal something so utterly personal to a stranger bespoke her desperation. No woman would lie about something so abhorrent. Most women he knew were ignorant of such obscene happenings.

"My parents knew beforehand and didn't care. In exchange for five thousand pounds, I was his." She flicked him a brief glance. "You see, Manifred needed to wed to inherit a sizable fortune, and my father's coffers were quite empty."

Pain and betrayal riddled her murmured words.

"But ye said ye've been widowed for two years." He studied her, watching every nuance for a hint of deceit. He detected none. "Why do ye need a position now? Is it because yer husband didna provide for ye as ye said earlier?"

The ravished gaze she turned upon him, her eyes a deep violet from some inner torment, stabbed him straight in the heart. He had the ridiculous impulse to sweep her into his arms and comfort her. To vow she'd never need fear again.

"Partially," she said, staring at some point behind his shoulder. "I've lived with my parents since shortly after he died."

That took him aback. If she was the widow of a wealthy man, why was she destitute?

Did he have a gambling problem?

Was she a spendthrift?

He raked a critical gaze over her ugly gown. If this

was an example of her wardrobe, she hadn't been frivolous in that regard, for certes.

"My father needed funds again. So once more, even though I'm of age and I objected most strenuously, he arranged another match for me. To a man even worse than Manifred."

God's bloody bones.

How was that possible?

She thrust her chin up, proud and defiant and glorious. "I'd have died before I allowed Leslie Warrington to touch me, the lecherous degenerate. Or before I permitted myself to be bought again. So I searched for a position, sold my possessions to pay for the journey, and fled without telling anyone where I went. That's why I used an assumed name."

That still didn't explain why she lived with her parents, but she'd revealed far more than he'd anticipated. Admiration thrummed through him for her bravery and daring. He didn't doubt her sordid tale. It astonished and liberated in an odd way.

He rose and stepped near her chair.

Berget eyed him suspiciously, a vulnerability in

her gaze that fueled his anger toward her parents and that Warrington slime. Clearly, she didn't trust Graeme, but she also silently pleaded for him to believe her.

Believe and trust. Not exactly the same thing. One could believe someone without trusting them.

He suspected she didn't trust anyone and had good reason not to. How awful it must've been for her to be at the whim of uncaring parents and a pervert for a husband.

What was it about this particular woman that called to him?

With an undefinable pressure behind his breastbone, he knelt on one knee beside her, using his thumb to wipe away the dampness on her petal-soft cheek.

"I believe ye."

But he'd be unwise to claim he trusted her yet, because he didn't. Not mere hours after meeting.

Wonder and relief widened her eyes, and she breathed, "You do? Truly?"

"Aye," He covered her small hands with one of

his. "And I vow to ye, I shall keep ye safe. Ye needna fear any longer. Ye're welcome at Killeaggian for as long as ye want to stay."

Her gorgeous eyes welled with moisture and, despite blinking several times, the tears spilled over onto her porcelain cheeks. "Thank you…Graeme."

Whether it was the use of his name, or that he couldn't bear to see her sorrow, or that he'd finally admitted the need to hold her in his arms prevailed above all else, but he leaned in and gathered her into his embrace.

He never could stand to see a woman cry. It eviscerated him, releasing a primal urge to soothe and coddle.

She gasped and stiffened as he encircled her, but he murmured, "Shh, *leannan. Cha tig cron sam bith thu a-nis.* Nae harm will come to ye now," into her ear as he rubbed the fine bones of her spine.

A shudder rippled through her small frame, followed by a gasping sob. "I'm sorry," she managed, trying to pull away, but he held her firm, whispering soothing words in Gaelic.

"Dinna be."

Finally, she slumped into him and wept.

Several moments passed before she collected herself. She blinked up at him, her lashes spikey, her nose red, and her cheeks damp. And Graeme swore by all the saints, he'd never seen a more exquisite face.

"Feelin' a wee bit better?" He brushed a stray tendril of dark honey-toned hair off her wet cheeks.

"Yes," she said, averting her face. "But I'm mortified to have come undone like that on my first day here. I don't normally cry."

With his forefinger, he turned her face back to his. "Ye've nothin' to be ashamed of, lass. I think ye've had a hard time of it and have been verra brave for a verra long time."

Her gaze shifted to his mouth before darting away, and awareness tingled through him, sparking his lust once more.

She desired *him.*

She was a widow with a widow's needs. And the Good Lord and all the saints knew his body hungered for her. Was ravenous for her. He'd been without a woman for months. Far too long.

Even as his mind screamed a warning, he leaned in and brushed his lips over hers.

God. So verra sweet.

She remained perfectly still for an instant before her mouth slackened and moved under his. Awkward and unsure.

Raging desire buffeted Graeme, igniting a wildfire in his blood so swiftly and powerfully, his head spun dizzyingly. He prodded the corner of her mouth with his tongue and, with a half-moan, half-sigh, she opened to him. When he touched his tongue to hers, she went taut, then after a brief hesitation, tentatively met his thrusts.

Damnation, if he didn't know better, he'd think her an untried maid. Had her husband never kissed her? Mayhap not. Had he used her as he did the boys he preferred?

Nae. Nae.

His mind screamed no to the revolting thought and to his taking advantage of her weakened emotional state.

This was wrong.

It went against all he stood for.

He was the laird.

Berget was a governess and was now under his protection. Which meant, she was forbidden to him. His honor dictated it as much as his word did. Taking care to keep his expression neutral, he set her from him and stood.

"Graeme?" Confusion shone in her eyes.

Despite his descent into stupidity, she must know her place. "Ye do give me reason to doubt ye're morally fit to school my nieces."

God damn ye for an arse, ye cold-hearted scunner.

Blanching as if slapped, her rosy mouth parted on a tiny gasp.

He recognized the instant her passion turned to chagrin, then glorious fury, for she swiftly pointed her attention to his boots. Her breathing shallow and rapid, her lips pressed into a thin ribbon, she held herself so stiffly she might shatter if he sneezed.

"I'll have bathwater sent up for ye. Tomorrow, I'll take ye on a tour of the keep and grounds." Without a backward glance, he strode from her chamber, leaving the door open.

9

Over the next week, Berget settled into a routine with her charges. After breakfast with their mother and uncle in the great hall, she spent the morning in the schoolroom. Camden had yet to return from Edinburgh, and she wasn't certain whether to be relieved or nervous.

With each passing day, she grew more attached to Cora and Elena, and more exasperated with Laird Graeme Kennedy, who all but ignored her.

Her pupils proved to be intelligent, eager to learn, but also spirited. Unaccustomed to sitting for lengthy stretches, the girls became restless after a couple of hours. If the weather permitted, Berget took the lasses for a lengthy walk before their midday meal. They visited the stables, gardens, even the family cemetery.

She used the opportunity to instruct them about flora and fauna and the climate.

When the weather prohibited them from venturing outdoors, she tutored them in needlework, music, etiquette and comportment, and even dance lessons. The latter was what they were engaged in at present.

Her back to the entrance, Berget demonstrated the first steps of the minuet while the girls imitated her movements.

"'Tis quite simple, girls. Four straight steps in any direction." Step. Step. Step. Step.

"When I add a Sink and Rise to the first step, 'tis called a Bouree." She dipped to show them.

"And when I add the Sink and Rise to the fourth step, 'tis called a Half Coupee." She sank again.

Humming, she demonstrated the entire process once more as Cora and Elena, their little faced pinched with concentration and limbs gangly, bobbled along across from her.

"Och, ye canna do it properly without a partner, lass."

She started and glanced behind her.

Graeme's large frame filled the doorframe, and from the amused grin slanting his mouth, he'd been observing her efforts for some time. As usual, he wore a belted plaid, a fine white linen shirt, long plaid waistcoat, and black neckerchief tied at his strong neck.

Today his woolen jacket was a dark blue and deepened his eye color to indigo. The fabric strained against his corded muscles, reminding her once more of his powerful build. Must he be so damned virile? So blatantly masculine?

The fury that had seized her that first night as he questioned her morality had gradually abated, leaving her more confused about him. *He'd* kissed her. True, she'd responded like a wanton and, after a restless night, admitted to herself that she'd been as much at fault as he.

Truth be told, he was within his rights to dismiss her, and that he hadn't gave her much to ponder. He'd abdicated his promise to take her on a tour of Killeaggian though. Instead, Lady Marjorie had done so.

Berget angled her head. "My laird."

She hid her satisfied smile as a line of disapproval appeared between his eyes. He couldn't very well insist she address him as Graeme in front of his nieces. Not if they were to observe propriety. Which he was most adamant must be adhered to.

In five sleek strides, he was at her side, extending his too-big hand. "Miss Jonston, please allow me to partner with ye."

Her pulse fluttered indecently in excitement. Stupid thing, flitting about like a covey of nervous quail.

He sounded the perfect gentleman. Did she detect a hint of lingering remorse in his piercing blue eyes?

Cora and Elena burst into fits of giggles.

"Uncle Graeme, ye canna dance a min-ette," Cora said, mispronouncing the word. "Ye only ken how to dance the sword dance and jigs."

Jigs? Berget couldn't imagine this brawny Highlander prancing about in such a manner.

"Nae, Cora. Ye're wrong," Elena argued. "He's danced at weddin's and such too."

Berget eyed him uncertainly, her stomach queerly tense. Except for meals—which surprisingly, she was expected to take with the family, as were the girls—he'd avoided her since sharing what, to her, had been a bone-melting kiss.

However, the kiss had been nothing but a cruel test to him. A test she'd failed most soundly. That knowledge still stung her pride. But she had learned her lesson. He wasn't to be trusted.

Oh, how she'd chided herself fiercely many times a day for being so utterly imprudent as to kiss him back. In all honesty, she'd expected him to pack her aboard a coach the next morning. Gratitude that he hadn't made her redouble her efforts to be an exceptional governess.

To her astonishment, she'd also found a politely worded note of apology slipped beneath her door the next morn. Graeme assured her his behavior was a mistake he deeply regretted and that she was safe from any further advances from him. He made no mention of his slur to her character.

Should she be insulted or relieved?

That niggling question she'd asked dozens of times the past week and was no closer to an answer than she had been upon reading the short missive.

"Miss Jonston?" he said once more, lifting his hand an inch.

With no viable excuse to refuse him, Berget addressed her rapt pupils. "Girls, before you begin dancing, always curtsy to your partner. He will bow to you."

She dipped, and Graeme bent at the waist, a wry smile quirking his bold mouth.

Both girls followed suit, though Cora's tongue sticking between her lips bespoke the effort it took her not to stumble.

He lightly gripped Berget's hand, and her heart fluttered against her ribs like the frantic wings of a snared sparrow. Oh, this wouldn't do. Not at all. She mustn't allow him to affect her. The frenzied flapping slowed to a manageable tremor.

Careful to keep her focus straight ahead, she proceeded through the steps with him. To her astonishment, he hummed—slightly off-key—which struck the girls as hysterical.

They clung to each other, laughing and pointing. And then once more, they awkwardly attempted to mimic the steps and movements.

"It does rather sting a mon's dignity to be the object of his nieces' amusement," he murmured from the side of his mouth.

Cutting him a sideways glance, her stomach pitched, and she missed a step upon seeing his devastating smile. Why, it almost looked compassionate. Tender even. "They adore you."

"Och, and I them."

He'd make a wonderful father.

The notion caused the most peculiar warmth to bud in her middle, burgeoning ever hotter and expanding outward. Was he considering marriage to Lady Marjorie? It made sense, considering how fond he was of his nieces. She had been the wife of the late laird, after all.

The earlier warmth disappeared, replaced by…well, she didn't know precisely what the peculiar feeling was. But it was wholly uncomfortable and just as unwelcome.

Clearing her throat, she cast an eye to the girls.

Hand in hand, they skipped and romped around, having completely abandoned their dancing lessons.

"Are ye still sore from yer fall?" Graeme inquired solicitously, drawing her to a stop but still holding her ungloved hand. His blue-eyed gaze swept her from head to foot, and a glint of appreciation darkened his eyes to cobalt, making her glad she'd worn her rose gown today.

Of the six she'd brought with her, this frock was her second favorite.

Not trusting herself to speak, and very much aware of the large, coarse fingers cradling hers, she shook her head. He'd already alluded she lacked morals. Holding her bare hand was most improper.

Was this another test?

Well, she'd not fail again if it was. She withdrew her hand and, after linking her fingers behind her back, said, "I'm quite recovered."

She wasn't. Bruises colored her bum and left shoulder.

A knowing look entered his eyes. Not quite

approval, but as if he knew she didn't mind his touch. "Ye will let Marjorie or me ken if ye need anythin'?"

"I have all that I require, thank you." She glanced to the doorway, half-expecting the kind lady to appear. "Lady Marjorie must've been anticipating a governess for her daughters for some time. The schoolroom is well stocked. I cannot imagine anything she hasn't thought of."

Did Berget dare ask to borrow books from the keep's absolutely wondrous library?

Her first day here, she'd taken her charges there, explaining to them that once they'd learned their letters, they could read any of the hundreds of books lining the dark wooden shelves.

Except for Cora and Elena's bedtime story—after which their uncles and mother bid them goodnight—and supervising the girls during supper, Berget's evenings were her own. She'd grown quite bored sitting alone in her chamber with nothing to do.

"Might I borrow a book from the library?" she asked on impulse.

It was his turn to look taken aback. "Of course. Ye

needna ask. This is yer home now. If ye're interested in a particular subject, I can point ye in the right direction. My grandfather had the books alphabetized by subject."

Appreciation squeezed her heart. Surely, that's all the sensation was. "Thank you, but I believe I can manage."

A governess who couldn't properly find her way around a library had no business teaching children.

Graeme clasped his arms behind his back too. "Has Marjorie approached ye about helpin' her with the plans for the *cèilidh* in three weeks? 'Tis to be a grand celebration."

Berget had never attended a *cèilidh*. She wasn't sure if she was expected to participate in the gathering either. She supposed there was time enough to ask that later.

He glanced to his nieces, who'd abandoned their dancing lessons to fuss over Frigg's eight wriggling puppies in a box near the hearth.

"She mentioned the celebration but said I had enough to keep me busy just attending to the lasses."

Berget couldn't prevent a longing look toward Frigg and her bairns. Mother had forbidden any pets. As an only child neglected by her parents, she'd been lonely and longed for a kitten or puppy.

Graeme must've caught her wistful sigh. He glanced between her and the mewling pups, born just two days ago. "Have ye held one yet?"

She jerked her attention to him. "No. I didn't know 'twas permitted."

He leveled her such an odd look, a flush worked its scorching way from her square bodice to her hairline.

"Come." Taking her arm, he led her to the straw-lined box Frigg lay in. At his approach, the deerhound wagged her tail excitedly. He squatted and rubbed her ears before running a hand down her back. "There's a bonnie lass."

Frigg's tail flopped faster. Her adoration was endearing and somewhat embarrassing.

"Sit down, Miss Jonston." He indicated a place beside the bed. "Is there a pup in particular ye'd like to hold?"

Sporting a crest-shaped white patch on her chest, a tiny puppy weakly lifted her head. "That one." Berget pointed as she settled to the floor. "She's much smaller than the others. Her mother won't mind?"

"Och, she's the runt, and nae, Frigg willna mind as long as she kens ye," he said, lifting the pup hardly larger than a small rat. "This wee lass will have to fight to survive. I'll watch her closely, and if she's no' growin' stronger, I'll have to supplement her milk."

"Poor darling," Berget crooned, kissing the puppy's silky head. "Aren't you the sweetest thing? I promise, we'll not let you die." She closed her eyes, bringing the tiny body to her neck.

"Uncle Graeme, can we hold a puppy too?" Elena asked.

"No' right now. Frigg will become upset if we take too many of her bairns from her at once. Besides, ye need to ken how to handle a wee pup first. Watch Miss Jonston and learn." After patting her shoulder, he sank to the floor beside Berget.

Cora and Elena crowded close, eyes wide in wonderment as they whispered all the ways they could help with the pups. They suggested several names as well, including Laird Graybeard, Cendrillon—from the fairytale they insisted Berget tell them every night—and Sir Barkley who had their uncle's forehead wrinkling in mirth.

That was how Lady Marjorie found them ten minutes later when she swept into the hall. "Miss Jonston?"

Her words and steps faltered upon spying a sleeping puppy in Berget's arms and Graeme's head near hers as he ran a big finger over the puppy's downy head.

Two neat lines furrowed Lady Marjorie's forehead as she looked between them. Something akin to hurt shadowed her face when her attention rested on him.

"What is happening?" she asked as she approached.

Graeme collected the sleeping puppy from Berget and returned her to her mother. "Miss Jonston and I are givin' the girls a lesson on responsibility."

"*Uh-hum.*" A wry auburn eyebrow arched as Lady Marjorie leveled him with what was clearly a disbelieving look. She then turned a speculative eye on Berget, as if seeing her clearly for the first time.

The keen assessment quickened Berget's guilt over the kiss that first night. She owed this woman much. Lady Marjorie couldn't believe anything untoward went on between Berget and Graeme. Still, she wasn't certain what to say to dispel the tension or suspicion in the air.

Finally, she decided to pretend not to notice. From her many years in Edinburgh society, she'd learned protesting innocence only served to inflame unwarranted interest.

The lady doth protest too much, methinks.

Precisely. Shakespeare had the right of it.

In one deft move, Graeme rose then offered Berget a hand. With Lady Marjorie staring on, she'd like to have refused, but she was also trying to teach her charges manners. Keeping her eyes lowered, she permitted him to assist her and then edged away murmuring, "Thank you."

Diffidence and demureness. Diffidence and demureness.

The other refrain she repeated a hundred times a day in her head.

"A letter arrived for you, Miss Jonston" Lady Marjorie extended the rectangle while bestowing a fond smile upon her daughters.

Alarm rendering her unable to move, Berget stared.

No one knew she was here.

Fear slithered up her spine, raising gooseflesh, and she swallowed.

Graeme stepped forward, taking the letter from Marjorie.

She narrowed her eyes the slightest but didn't object.

"Why dinna ye take it to yer chamber and read in private?" he suggested, sliding the rectangle into Berget's icy hand and wrapping her fingers around its length.

"Yes. I shall do so later." She marshaled her composure and summoned a tremulous smile, tucking the missive into her bosom. At once, she regretted doing so since the movement drew Graeme's attention to the modest show of flesh above her bodice. "I promised the girls a painting lesson—"

"It can wait," he said gently.

Was she so very transparent?

His consideration touched her, but also enhanced her guilt. She'd told him everything except about the journal and falsifying her letters of recommendation.

Again, Marjorie swept her astute glance between them and, this time, perception widened her eyes the merest bit. Pain and understanding flickered in their pretty brown depths. Nonetheless, the epitome of kindness, she offered a gentle smile. "Girls, Maive told me she tested a new black bun recipe. Would you like to sample a piece?"

At once, amid squeals of delight, the lasses launched to their feet and each clasped one of their mother's hands.

"Only a small slice, darlings," she said. "I don't want you to ruin your appetites before dinner."

The guilt prodding Berget sank its talons deeper.

Lady Marjorie was a most perceptive woman.

At the doorway, she glanced over her shoulder, a

soft smile playing around the corners of her mouth. "Graeme, there's also correspondences for you in your study. One is from Camden."

Berget couldn't dispel the feeling something significant had occurred, but what, she couldn't fathom.

"If you will excuse me, please." With a brief nod to Graeme, she hurried to her comfortably appointed chamber. In shades of blue and ivory, she found it refreshing and soothing at the same time.

She went to stand before the window.

No fire burned in the hearth, and she didn't want to take the time to light a taper. The single, narrow window afforded the only light in her room. Forcing air into her lungs, she withdrew the letter from her bodice and pried her stiff fingers open to examine the missive.

It was from the agency that had hired her.

Anticipation and trepidation vied for supremacy as the air stalled in her lungs.

Her breath left her in a whoosh, and she broke the wax seal. Swiftly reading the short note, she scrunched her nose and wrinkled her forehead. Two men had visited the registry asking several questions about her.

The agency expressed concern that Berget had mislead them to gain her position.

Two men?

For certain Camden was one. But who, in God's holy name, was the other? Father?

She brought a shaky hand to her forehead, suddenly feeling sick and lightheaded. Had the employment registry also written to Lady Marjorie or Graeme with their suspicions?

10

Unable to sleep after reading Camden's letter this afternoon, Graeme had spent the evening sequestered in the library. The mantel clock chimed one in the morning, and he brushed a hand over his bleary eyes.

The fire burned low in the grate as he fingered the whisky glass he held in his left hand. As he was wont to do when alone, he'd rolled his shirtsleeves up. His waistcoat, jacket, and neckcloth lay flung across another chair.

Thor, Vidar, and Freya lay sprawled before the fading fire, their soft snores and rhythmic breathing an accompaniment to the clock's gently *tick-tock*.

Never before had he been so damned conflicted. Not even when he'd made the difficult decision to stay neutral during the Jacobite Rising. Sion had just died, and the last thing his clan had needed was more heartache.

Since her arrival, Berget had turned his well-ordered life upside down; arse over chin upside down.

Pleading a fierce headache, she'd asked to be excused from dining with the family tonight. Whatever her letter had contained, it had upset her enough to keep her in her chamber.

Always compassionate, Marjorie had agreed and, at once, sent an herbal tea concoction of some sort to Berget's chamber, along with a dinner tray and the order for bathwater scented with lavender oil.

Graeme hadn't missed the pain whisking across Marjorie's features today when she'd seen him and Berget together. He couldn't explain, even to himself, why the young widow drew him the way she did or the complex emotions she kindled. Emotions he didn't want to feel, much less examine closely.

It was an almost irresistible force he could neither name nor pretend to comprehend. His spirit was inexorably woven together with Berget's.

It made no sense...was illogical, impractical, and possibly risky.

But mayhap now Marjorie would finally understand he would never return her regard. He loved her as a sister. Nothing more.

Drumming the pads of his fingers on his thigh, he stared unseeing into the glowing embers.

Camden's letter verified most of what Berget had already disclosed.

While that relieved him and raised her in his estimation, for she'd been truthful with him in part, Camden's investigation also revealed her letters of recommendation were likely forged. No such persons as the Honorable Hortensia Millikan or Ladies Charlotte McLendon and Patrice Ferguson were known to anyone Camden had questioned in Edinburgh.

That left Graeme with a difficult decision, one that left him wholly conflicted.

Berget performed her duties with exemplary skill and care. The lasses already adored her, and although it was probably too soon for her to forge a friendship with Marjorie, the women shared mutual respect for one another.

In the short time Berget had been part of the keep, he'd come to look for her throughout the day. He soundly cursed himself for a fool each time he did, however.

Permitting his eyelids to drift shut, Graeme pressed two fingers to the bridge of his nose.

What would he have done had he been in her position?

Facing another unbearable marriage, and with despicable parents who had no care for her feelings or desires? As a single female, to venture out on her own the way Berget had proved she had fortitude and was resourceful. It also demonstrated she was capable of scheming, secrecy, and subterfuge.

Not exactly qualities prized in a governess.

She'd also lied to Marjorie and the registry office. But then again, who could she have asked for references? For surely anyone Berget had approached would've questioned her reasons and quite probably have alerted her parents.

A muffled oath passed his lips. Had she misled him about other things too? Did the outcome she desired excuse the methods she'd used?

Had anyone truly been hurt by her deceit?

Didn't that remain to be seen?

While he didn't condone Berget's deception—for he truly valued honesty—he did understand the decision she'd made. But...could he, should he, continue to employ a known dissembler?

He hadn't missed the absolute terror flitting across her face when Marjorie presented her with the letter. That revealed how much she truly dreaded marrying Warrington. Perhaps Camden ought to look into that blackguard's background as well.

Opening his eyes, Graeme turned his mouth upward.

Aye, that's exactly what he would have his brother do. In the meanwhile, he'd keep silent and continue to deliberate what to do about Berget Jonston. And, by Odin's teeth, wrangle his burgeoning feelings and desire for the luscious widow under control.

He was damned curious to know what her letter contained, however.

Marjorie had mentioned it was from the registry office she'd used to hire Berget. Interesting. Also, a trifle disturbing. Had the agency warned her that Camden was snooping about?

Perhaps it was time to have another candid conversation with her. Before the girls became any more attached. Before *he* did.

He wouldn't turn her onto the street, of course. He wasn't that cold-hearted. Though he owed her nothing, if he did indeed decide to terminate her employment, he would provide her enough coin to sustain her for a few months.

His stomach turned at the notion, and he quaffed back the remaining whisky, welcoming the slow, sharp burn to his gut. The truth was, he didn't want Berget to leave. Not yet anyway. She fascinated and intrigued him; he wanted to know her better.

To see her rare smiles and the sweet way she crooned over the puppies. To watch her interactions with the lasses, and hear her light, unfettered laughter.

How could a woman he'd met hardly more than a week ago have burrowed under his skin, invaded his every thought, and, he feared, touched his heart so profoundly?

Graeme was no stranger to beautiful women, so why didn't he find his normal self-discipline lapsing? His perpetual state of semi-arousal might be to blame in part, but he'd never before let his carnal urges interfere with duty.

He'd like to take her riding—to show her his lands, introduce her to the villagers and crofters. He wanted to dance with her at the celebration. Just the thought of touching her brought the expected swell to his nether regions.

No proper governess participated in such activities, and certainly no laird in his right mind would consider asking her to. But he'd found since meeting the captivating Mrs. Berget Jonston that his mind rather ignored common sense. His body too.

Sighing, he set the glass on the side table and shoved to his feet.

He was Laird of Killeaggian Tower.

It was in his sole discretion whether she stayed or left. At present, he was of the inkling to retain her for the indefinite future, despite her ruses. As long as his nieces were not at risk, that was.

Nevertheless, a conversation with Berget tomorrow wouldn't be amiss.

Concern for the smallest pup in Frigg's litter niggling, he made his way to the great hall.

As he'd done the past two nights, and as he instructed a serving girl to do several times during the day, he gently removed the seven larger, stronger puppies from their mother, and encouraged the frail one to nurse until her wee belly was full.

He'd always had a penchant for the underdog, for those down on their fortunes and in need. Likely, that explained his proclivity toward Berget too.

Ballocks.

Frigg whined, straining to see her babies cradled between Graeme's crossed legs. He soothed her with a few soft words. "Dinna fash yerself, lass. I'm tryin' to save yer bairn's life."

If he must, he'd supplement the pup's milk intake with goat milk.

If Berget stayed on, he'd like to make a gift of the pup to her.

Och, ye've already made up yer mind, ye clot head. Who are ye tryin' to fool?

From the corner of his eye, he saw a movement at the hall's entrance. Careful not to jostle the sleeping puppies, he turned his head.

Berget stood there, her uneasiness tangible.

In the flickering firelight, her russet hair appeared more chestnut-hued. It hung freely about her slender shoulders and back, and she fiddled with a thick strand near her collarbone. Belted at the waist, her chaste white night robe gave her an angelic appearance.

Though this woman had been married, there was an innocent air about her. A gentleness too that came from having suffered much, and rather than becoming bitter and hard, she'd endured adversity with enviable grace.

As it did whenever she was near, his pulse quickened, and he couldn't prevent his appreciative smile at the innocent seductress.

"I was worried about the puppy," she offered by way of an explanation. "Though, I don't know what I intended to do."

He motioned her inside. "She's just finished nursin'."

She glided across the stone floor, her feet scarcely making a sound. It was then he noticed her bare toes peeking from beneath her night rail.

A smile hitched his mouth.

Even Marjorie didn't toddle about the keep barefoot, and that the prim and proper governess should delighted him.

The soft angled planes of her face pearly in the muted light, she folded gracefully to her knees. She leaned over the enclosure and tentatively touched the smallest pup upon her back. "She's tiny, but she seems strong. She has a determined spirit."

Nodding, he permitted his gaze to feast upon the lush mounds straining against the vee of her bodice. It occurred to him, instantly making him hard as marble, that she was likely naked beneath her night shift.

Thumping her tail once, Frigg licked Berget's hand. "She likes ye. All the dogs do as a matter of fact."

Berget slid him a brief glance, then lifted a

delicate shoulder. "I like animals. Especially horses and dogs." She brushed her forefinger over the puppy once more. "If she were mine, I'd name her Bia. She was the Greek goddess of power, might, and physical strength."

It was on the tip of his tongue to tell her that the pup was hers if she liked, but he checked the impulse. It was too soon to make that kind of a promise. It suggested she'd be here for a long while. Instead, he gently returned the other puppies to their anxious mother, who promptly set to grooming them.

A gentle smile framing her mouth, Berget watched, entranced. "She has eight babies, yet she takes such gentle care with each. I know human mothers who cannot be bothered to spend time with their one or two offspring."

Her own mother?

Given the wistfulness of her tone, faintly tinged with regret and disappointment, he'd vow he'd hit the target dead center. Everything he'd witnessed thus far suggested she'd be a superb mother. A yearning, unlike anything he'd ever experienced prior to this moment to see her cradling her bairn to her breast buffeted him.

He was fast losing control of—*everything*—when it came to her.

Dangerous. Foolish. And not to be tolerated.

"I never asked ye before. Do ye have brothers or sisters?" He rested his hand atop the whelping bed, slicing her a brief side-eyed glance.

She gave a short shake of her head as she sank onto her heels before gathering her hair and twisting it into a thick rope across her left shoulder. "No. I had a sister, but she died two years before I was born."

Perhaps if she'd had a brother or sister, her parents mightn't have used her as a human pawn. *Och, nae.* People of their ilk likely would have exploited all of their children.

She touched the scar on the back of his hand. Then as if she realized her forwardness, promptly pulled her hand away, pink tinging her cheeks. "How did you come by that?"

Chuckling, he raised his hand so they both could see the jagged ridge more clearly. "'Tis no' a tale of bravery or chivalry. I was helpin' to dislodge a stuck wagon when the wheel suddenly shattered. A piece wedged into my hand."

Her mouth softened and formed an O. Swiftly, her gaze darted between his hand and his face. "Did it hurt terribly?"

"Nae." He hitched a shoulder. "I've had worse."

He had the scars to prove it.

A comfortable silence settled upon them, the fire snapping in the hearth, and the sweet snuffling sounds of the puppies filling the atmosphere. After several peaceful moments, she sighed. "Well, I should bid you goodnight. 'Tis awfully late." She scrunched her nose. "Or early, I suppose," she quipped.

As Berget shifted to rise, Graeme encircled her delicate wrist with his hand, and she cast him a questioning glance. No alarm but simply inquiry shone in her guileless gaze.

"What was in yer letter? I ken it frightened ye, else I wouldna ask."

At once, her gaze sank to the floor, and her tongue darted out, moistening her lower lip. Tension radiated off her in undulating waves.

She was afraid. *Nae, terrified.*

"Ye can tell me, lass," he said with gentle encouragement. "I promise, I strive to always be fair."

Her eyelids fluttered shut, dark fans against her pale cheeks. A shuddery sigh whispered past her pink lips.

"The registry office notified me that two men have been inquiring after me." She opened her amethyst eyes, luminous in their desolation. "I accidentally overheard you in the drawing room telling your brother to investigate me. I understand your reasons. In fact, if I were in your position, I'd likely do the same."

"I didna expect ye to confess all to me that first night," he said simply. It was the truth. "We were strangers, after all. Who is the other mon?"

She lifted a slender shoulder. "I honestly don't know. Mayhap my father, and that tells me he's truly desperate for the funds Warrington promised him for my hand. I wonder if he's in some sort of trouble?"

Graeme would wager on it.

A bitter laugh escaped her as she toyed with the

ends of her hair. "Isn't it ironic that most women of my station must provide a dowry in order to wed? Yet somehow, my father has been able to find two men willing to pay him a substantial sum to marry me. Doesn't that say something about the caliber of the men he promised me to?"

Indeed, it did. And it also said much, much more about the character of her feckless father.

Berget Jonston was a treasure. A rare and priceless jewel. A gem to be protected and cherished. Not a commodity to be sold to the highest bidder.

Graeme canted his head. "Camden also said he suspects yer references were forged."

Her tongue made another brief appearance, and she gave a cautious nod, her face wreathed with uncertainty. "They are."

It didn't surprise him that she admitted to the falsehood. He'd come to expect forthrightness from her and, so far, she'd been frank when questioned directly.

Her beautiful gaze pleading for understanding, she laid a palm on his forearm. "I had no one to ask. No one to write them for me. And even if I did, that would've left a trail. My father, and perhaps Warrington, would've found me in short order. In fact, I now fear they will in any event."

"'Tis possible for certain," he agreed.

He'd not lie to her about the likelihood. She needn't fret, however. He'd vowed to protect her and protect her he would as long as she resided in his keep. The question was, how long would she be there?

Her voice trembled as she struggled to maintain her composure, moisture glinting in her violet eyes. "I understand I canna remain here now. I ken 'tis a lot to ask ye, but would ye permit me a couple of days to send a letter? I have a friend, Arieen Wallace—"

"Coburn's wife?"

"Aye," she agreed. "Do ye ken him?"

She'd slipped into a brogue again. Something, he noted, she only did when highly agitated.

A charred log fell, sending a billow of sparks up the chimney. "I do. Why would ye write her?"

"To ask if I might come to stay with her for a while."

"Nae, I canna permit it."

She went perfectly still before her shoulders slumped, and she tucked her chin to her chest. "I...I understand. I'll leave in the mornin'."

"Nae, lass. Ye willna." He raised her chin with a fingertip. "I dinna want ye writin' her, because I canna ensure yer safety at Lockelieth. I told ye, I would protect ye. I can only do that here."

"I'm sorry, Graeme," she whispered, dashing at the tears glistening on her wan cheeks. "I didna ken what else to do, and now I've become a burden to ye."

He uncrossed his legs, and with a sigh of resignation, wrapped an arm about her shoulders, tucking her to his side. "Aye, mayhap with yer deception, but I understand yer reasons. Thus far, ye've diligently performed yer duties, and I have nae complaints. Marjorie is thrilled to have ye here, and so are the lasses."

Without thinking, he laid his cheek atop her silky hair and skimmed his fingers up and down her arm. Embracing her was as natural as breathing. He feared he'd come to need to touch her every bit as much as his body required oxygen to live.

She snuggled into his side like a trusting kitten desperate for the comfort he offered.

"I would ken, lass, do ye harbor any more secrets I should ken about?" He spoke into her hair, inhaling her unique, intoxicating scent. She smelled of heather and lavender, no doubt from her bath.

Tilting her head in the crook of his arm, a fine line appeared between Berget's eyebrows.

"Aye. There was a book. A secret journal of sorts. It contained the names of the patrons who frequented an...*unsavory* establishment in Edinburgh."

He could well imagine precisely what sort of establishment.

Her eyelids drifted down for a moment before she bravely met his gaze once more. "Manifred's name was listed, and I don't know who all else." She swallowed her abhorrence of the subject, clearly at odds with her need to reveal what she knew. "There was a dreadful scandal when the journal somehow made its way before the king."

"Christ on the cross," Graeme swore.

King George I was not well liked, particularly by the Scots. No doubt, the journal she spoke of revealed the names of more than one Scottish laird. The king would relish the power and control such a revolting find would afford him.

"What happened?" He turned his attention to the tempting hollow beneath her shell-like ear. He nuzzled her there, smiling when she gasped. So soft, like warm silk.

"The king seized the properties of some of the people recorded in the journal." Her voice, now a husky contralto, quavered slightly. "Others were executed. Manifred had died by the time the scandal broke, but his estate and fortune—"

"Were forfeited to good ol' George." He lifted his head from his sensual explorations. "That's why ye returned to yer parents' household."

"Aye." Her raspberry-toned lips parted on a raspy chuckle. "I seem to have been born under a bad omen. Trouble follows me like my own shadow."

"The trouble ye speak of is no' of yer own doin', and I'm verra glad ye're here." He was, but he was daft to admit to the weakness.

Astonishment crinkled her glorious amethyst eyes as she stared at him. Eyes he could wade into and drown and not care that he'd died in their jeweled depths.

"Because Cora and Elena needed a governess?" She toyed with the ends of her hair.

"Nae, *leannan*," he murmured as he dipped his head lower, knowing even as he did so, he shouldn't.

Then his lips met hers, and when she eagerly opened her mouth, he was utterly and hopelessly lost. Like a scuttled ship foundering in the ocean, he sank into her sensual calling. He cupped the curve of her ribs, pulling her closer still as he ravaged her sweet mouth.

I'm glad ye're here, because even though I didn't ken it, I needed ye.

11

Berget wasn't even entirely sure how it came to be that the next morning, rather than schooling Cora and Elena in handwriting, reading, and mathematics, she sat atop a gentle mare as Graeme gave her a tour of his estate. At some point between the breath-stealing kisses and tantalizing caresses last night, she vaguely remembered agreeing to spend the morning with him.

Lady Marjorie hadn't seemed surprised when he'd announced at breakfast that rather than Berget conducting her governess' duties, she would accompany him on his weekly inspections and then to the village to become acquainted with the locals.

She mightn't know exactly how things were done in the Highlands, but Berget was fairly certain his request was beyond exceptional. As a widow, she didn't require a chaperon, but she couldn't prevent her troubling thoughts.

What would others think of her gallivanting around the countryside unescorted? Surely it would arouse speculation. And bring attention to her, which she could ill-afford.

"That's perfectly fine. I think it a good idea, in fact." Lady Marjorie agreed with what Berget had no doubt was a falsely cheery smile. "The girls are to have a fitting for their new gowns in the village, in any event."

They were?

This was the first Berget had heard of it.

Comprehension dawned, and she applied herself to pushing her eggs around her plate.

Lady Marjorie was attempting to save face.

Compassion welled within Berget, along with a good deal of guilt that this kind woman should be embarrassed or made uncomfortable. That she didn't aim any barbed looks or comments in Berget's direction only convinced her further that Lady

Marjorie was as beautiful inside as she was out.

A forkful of sausage halfway to his mouth, Graeme paused and quirked a skeptical brow. "Ye're havin' the lasses gowns made in the *village*?"

Marjorie pulled her attention away from wiping a dab of strawberry preserves from Cora's face and gave a casual nod. "Yes. I simply don't have time to sew new gowns with everything else I'm doing to prepare for the celebration. 'Tis but two weeks away."

Was there a hint of censure there?

Berget had offered to help more than once, and Lady Marjorie had dismissed her suggestions. Or was her comment directed toward Graeme?

Did she imply that he'd neglected his duties in some way?

"Aye, ye do have yer hands full." He relieved the fork of the sausage and, as he chewed, pointed that utensil in her general direction. "Do ye wish me to hire extra help from the village, or are there some items Miss Jonston might assist ye with?"

Lady Marjorie gave him a tolerant smile as if she addressed a lad and not the laird of the keep. "We've plenty of servants here, and as I've expressed to Miss Jonston already that she was hired to be a governess, not my companion or a maid."

Now that definitely held a starchy edge, not that Berget blamed the gentle lady. She'd obviously discerned that there was a connection between Graeme and Berget that neither seemed able to resist. Unlike the ladies she'd known in England and even in Edinburgh, Lady Marjorie handled her disappointment with a grace and aplomb Berget could only admire.

Nonetheless, she couldn't dismiss the surge of discomfit when Lady Marjorie turned her pretty dark eyes on Berget. "May I assume you'll be back this afternoon for music and French lessons?"

It wasn't so much a question as an expectation. After all, Berget was here to instruct the girls, not flit about the countryside with the laird. Her teacup in hand, she peered over the rim toward Graeme, silently asking if they would be back in time.

"I expect we'll return by early afternoon." His astute attention flickered between the two women and two lines creased his forehead. "But since ye'll be in the village too, and I plan on introducin' Miss Jonston to several of the merchants, why dinna we plan on havin' our midday meal together at The Stag and Hound?"

Cora fairly bounced in her seat with excitement. "Can we, Mama?"

"We've never dined there before," Elena said by way of explanation. She too looked expectantly at her mother.

A contemplative expression on her face, Marjorie swept her regard from Graeme to Berget, then to each of her daughters in turn. Her mouth turned up at the corners, the joy not quite reaching her eyes. "I think 'tis a perfect opportunity for my darlings to apply some of the decorum lessons they have been learning."

Hiding a wince, Berget sent up a silent prayer that her charges would remember at least some of what she'd been attempting to teach them this past week. Honestly, she'd barely begun their etiquette instruction.

Now, two hours later, attired in her royal blue riding habit, she tilted her face upward, savoring the sun's rays. Thank goodness she'd elected to keep the habit. She'd been tempted to sell the garment.

It would've fetched a fair price, but how would she have instructed her pupils how to seat a horse without it? For certain not attired in one of her day gowns, her calves and ankles exposed.

A large bird of some sort soared overhead in wide, lazy circles.

She breathed deeply of the invigorating, pure, clean Highland air. Far more pleasant than Edinburgh's fetid odors.

She liked it here.

Liked the simple, pleasant life.

Much more than she'd anticipated, and the brawny man a few feet away had much to do with her unexpected happiness.

Lord, his kisses last night.

Even now, she tingled in unmentionable places at the searing memories. Manifred's touches had gagged her, left her wanting to scrub her skin. But Graeme's made her want to shuck her pride. Her reservations. And her clothing. Not necessarily in that order.

She'd not have believed her body could respond so very differently with the two men.

Graeme drew Manannán to a halt near a craggy outcrop. A spectacular view of the meadows and fields below met her perusal. Killeaggian Tower loomed majestically on the far side, its stones glistening grandly in the mid-morning sunlight. To the west, nestled against a picturesque mountain backdrop, sat Killinkirk, like something from a painting.

They headed to the quaint village now, and she was saddened that this time alone with him must end.

"'Tis truly beautiful." Berget swept her gaze across the landscape once more. "Except for the two years I was married and lived in England, I've spent my life in Scotland. But I never ventured farther north than Edinburgh. I begin to understand why Highlanders are loath to leave here, despite the harsher clime and landscape."

Proudly assessing the lands before him, Graeme gave a slow nod. He wore no hat, but he'd tied his hair back into a queue with a black ribbon. The reddish streaks in his hair glinted coppery with the motion.

"Och. I could never leave. The Highlands are in my blood. My verra bones."

"I didn't know him, of course, but I believe your brother would be proud of you." Had Sion been as noble and confident as Graeme? "Especially how wonderful you've been to his daughters and wife."

She fiddled with the reins and bit her lower lip in indecision.

Was he aware of Lady Marjorie's feelings for him?

Glancing upward through her lashes, she caught him brazenly assessing her. A sweet, pleasant warmth like heated rose oil spread from her taut stomach, past her ribs—behind which her heart thumped an irregular rhythm—over her shoulders, and to her face, setting her cheeks aflame.

"I made him a vow on his deathbed, and I never break my oaths." His gaze held hers, mesmerizing and intense.

She couldn't look away. Didn't want to break the unnamable but compelling connection between them.

He'd promised to keep her safe, and that she could

remain at Killeaggian Tower for as long as she liked. But that was before he knew she'd forged her letters of recommendation. Would Lady Marjorie be of the same mind? Berget was quite certain he hadn't yet told his sister-in-law of her deception.

"I've been testing new crops and have also introduced a new breed of beef cattle called Galloways." He chuckled and pulled on his ear. "I've even planted potatoes like our Irish friends, and I'll tell ye, I received nae small amount of jestin' for the decision." He lifted a massive shoulder. "They're cheap to grow and are a good staple for the tenants' larders."

Head angled, Berget studied him. "You care for your tenants too, don't you?"

This man had a big heart and, not for the first time, she wondered why at nine-and-twenty he'd never married. Then, before she could tame her cursed tongue, the question spilled from her mouth.

"Graeme, why haven't you wed? You obviously adore children..."

She faltered at the searing look he speared her,

regretting her impulsiveness at once. He didn't appear angry exactly but rather guarded.

"Forgive me." She turned her attention to the reins clenched in her hands, wishing she could take back the words. "That was impertinent, and 'tis none of my business."

Wordlessly, he turned his horse toward the village. As she followed, her spirits sank. She'd crossed a line, though she wasn't sure what triggered his aloof response. They rode for several minutes, only the horses' hoofbeats and an occasional bird call interrupting the stilted silence.

Without warning, he reached out and seized the mare's halter, bringing both horses to a stop. His expression oddly devoid of emotion, he patted Manannán's creamy neck. "I was married."

Her gaze collided with his, her mouth parting in astonishment.

"Nine years ago. Her name was Nairna."

Something in his tone and the flash in his azure eyes warned her. This wasn't something he spoke of. In fact, no one at the keep had so much as breathed a word, and there could be no good reason for that. If she'd been a beloved wife, would there have been a reason to never mention her name?

"What happened?" she dared to ask, fearing his answer and his anger, yet willing to risk both to know him better.

Graeme glanced around, then led their horses beneath a thick copse of beech trees. A squirrel scolded from high on a branch, and a red deer bolted from the shelter, fleeing with graceful bounces.

He dismounted and, as always, she marveled at his athleticism.

After tying his steed's reins, he lifted Berget from her horse. He didn't release her but stood perfectly still, his eyes closed and a muscle ticking in his jaw as he struggled with his memories.

Berget touched his granite-hard arm, almost flinching at the tension radiating from him. "Graeme?"

His eyelids flickered open, the blue of his eyes like that after a winter's squall. A tempest yet churned within their stormy depths, and a sickening feeling rose from her belly to her throat.

"The subject clearly distresses you," she said. "I went beyond the mark by asking. Please don't feel the need to explain to me—"

He put his rough forefinger to her lips. "'Tis no' a pretty or romantic tale, Berget, but I'll tell ye. If ye want to ken."

"I want to know everything about you. But only if you wish to tell me." She clasped his hand between hers and pressed it to her chest.

"I've no' spoken of it ever. No' even to Sion or Marjorie. They ken bits and pieces, but no' the whole sordid thing." Jaw hard as steel, he gently withdrew his hand and stepped away.

What awfulness had occurred to do this to him?

She'd never known a braver, stronger man, but whatever he wanted to tell her made him hesitant and dread filtered into her veins.

His hands behind him, he rested his spine against a nearby tree. "Neither of us wanted to wed. She had just seen her seventeenth birthday, and I was but twenty. Nevertheless, our fathers wished the union to strengthen our clans. As Sion was already married, as the second eldest son, the responsibility fell to me."

Berget knew full well what it was like to marry to please a parent. And she also was aware of just how devasting such a match could be. Perhaps that was why Graeme had been gentle with her when he'd learned of her forced marriage and that she faced another despised match.

He pointed his attention overhead, speaking in a dispassionate monotone. "From her sixth birthday, Nairna had been raised in a French convent. She'd wanted to take her vows and was livid at being forced to return to Scotland, much less to wed a stranger."

Poor girl.

"I was young and angry at havin' my hand forced. Nonetheless, I did my utmost to be patient and kind. Still, she loathed me." He sighed, his mouth turning down as he traveled back in time in his mind. "Despised our…joinin's even more."

A slight shudder ran through him.

How could any woman despise coupling with this man?

A maiden herself, Berget's imagination had been

working overtime since she'd arrived at the keep. More than one night had included a delicious, erotic dream with him. If the act was anything like the glorious sensations he'd previously ignited in her, she'd be hard put not to seek out his bed.

He dipped his gaze to hers, and such agony reflected in his cloudy, tortured blue eyes that Berget gasped. She couldn't help but rush to his side and clasp his arm, needing to offer him comfort since she'd been the one to waken these horrid memories.

"Oh, Graeme, you needn't tell me anything more. I can see it causes you great pain and, once again, I beg you to forgive me for prying."

She did understand. Truly she did.

Just as speaking of Manifred always upset her when she'd much prefer to put that ugliness behind her and not dwell on the unchangeable past.

A wry half-smile kicked Graeme's mouth up on one side. He traced her jawline with his fingertip, and it was all she could do not to wrap her arms around his waist and lay her cheek against his broad chest. "*Jo*, ye've risked sharin' dark secrets with me. Ye might as well ken the whole story. If anyone can understand, I believe it would be ye."

Then, as if reading her very thoughts, he drew her against him, and as he had last night, rested his chin upon the crown of her head.

They fit together so perfectly, as if they were opposites sides of the same mold.

Did he feel it too? This undefinable pull, like magnets drawn together?

Sighing, she snuggled closer. This felt so natural and good. As if the whole world could pass them by, and as long as they held each other, everything would be all right in the end.

"I was overjoyed when Nairna told me she was expectin', even though she made it clear she was no' happy about her condition. She vowed she'd hate the child I'd given her."

Oh, God. How can anyone hate a bairn?

His ragged sigh sent a jagged crack right down the center of Berget's heart. Such anger welled in her. She pressed her lips into a tight line lest she say something unforgivable about an unhappy young woman she didn't know.

"But even as a young mon, I ken I wanted children," he murmured into her hair. "Throughout the pregnancy, despite the midwife's reassurances, her fears about givin' birth grew. When her time came, she was hysterical and inconsolable. I was much relieved when her labor was short, and overjoyed when she delivered a beautiful, wee lad."

She felt him swallow and glanced up to see tears shimmering in his eyes. One trickled from the corner, and he swiped it away.

"Nairna refused to hold the bairn, wouldna even look at him. She swore I'd never touch her again, that couplin' was the vilest of sins, and she wanted to vomit every time I came to her." His voice a rasping whisper, he went on. "She threw herself from the battlements that night."

Och, my God! My God!

Tears seeped from Berget's tightly squeezed eyes, and she stuffed a fist to her mouth to keep from crying out in anguish. To stifle the horror spiraling around and around in her middle. Sickening. Appalling. Incomprehensible.

"I vowed then I'd never marry again, and I've no' touched a respectable woman since. Until ye." His arms tightened around her as if he needed the comfort she provided him at that moment. "I named my son Andrew, but a mere week after enterin' this world, my wee laddie died." He uttered the strangled words as if he could barely get them off his tongue.

Berget's tears flowed freely now.

He'd suffered mightily too.

No wonder he adored his nieces so much.

"You should marry and have children, Graeme. It might help you heal."

"Och. Nae. I'll never consider weddin' again." He gave a vehement shake of his head. "When a woman despises yer touch that much, it does somethin' to ye. Makes somethin' inside ye shrivel and wither. And die."

How could it not?

He firmed his mouth into a taut line

"Besides, I dinna have to wed. Camden can inherit the lairdship." Graeme bore that burden too. "If he marries and has a son, our line will no' die out." He finally drew his gaze downward, regret and grief etched sharply on the sculpted planes of his face. "Nonetheless, I admit, Berget, *mo chridhe*, at times, I long for a child of my own."

His sweet. He'd called her his sweet.

Hope, undeserved and unbidden, welled within her.

"I do understand, Graeme, for I long for a child as well."

With all of my heart and soul.

She spoke into his jacket, the fabric muffling her words. She turned her face upward and cupped his cheek. "But I never suffered the loss of a son, so I shan't even pretend to appreciate your pain."

With a harsh growl, he claimed her mouth.

His previous kisses had been gentle and tentative, filled with sensual promise. This was a kiss of a wounded man desperate to find solace. To forget the memories haunting him. He gripped her buttocks, yanking her against the hardness of his groin as he ground his mouth over hers and ground his pelvis against her womanly softness.

Rather than frighten or disgust her, his unfettered passion set loose an equally unrestrained carnal desire in her. Want flooded her, heating her veins and pooling between her legs. She stood on her tiptoes, desperate to get closer to him, to convey she desired him every bit as much as he did her.

He rucked up her gown, the air whisking over her bare flesh before he lifted her, wrapping her thighs around his waist.

She ought to be shocked and appalled, but she wasn't. She ought to object to his scandalous overtures, but she reveled in them, hungry and eager for what he might do next.

This wild, untamed scoundrel sparked an answering need in her. If he wanted to take her here, right now, beneath these rustling trees, she hadn't the willpower to deny him.

The squirrel still chattering its outrage would get an eyeful though.

His hot lips abandoned her mouth, trailing kisses across her jaw, down her neck, nipping at her collarbone. His breath came ragged, uneven, and hoarse as he kneaded her buttocks with one large hand

and caressed her aching, swollen breast with the other.

"Och, lass. What ye do to me," he groaned against the hollow of her throat. "Ye ken I want ye as I've never wanted another."

What he did to *her*. This thing was wild and wonderful, and she never wanted it to end.

One of the horses snorted, stamping his feet, and Graeme went perfectly still.

"Shite, what am I doin'?" He slowly lowered her to the ground and pressed his forehead against hers. "Lass, I dinna ken what ye do to me, but I lose all self-restraint when ye are near. Ye've bewitched me, for certain. I swore after Nairna, I would control my lust. That never again would I impose myself on a gentle-bred woman."

She attempted a wobbly smile as she straightened her skirts, her knees more than a bit unsteady. "You didn't do anything I didn't want you to, Graeme. I enjoyed everything you did to me."

He needed to know that.

To know a respectable woman could crave his touch.

His gaze probed hers, searching, earnest, and

slightly puzzled. He raked his fingers through his hair, now hanging loosely about his shoulders. The ribbon holding the strawberry-blond strands back had come loose. He heaved a gusty sigh, reserve setting over his features once more as he took her by the elbow.

Nae. Dinna shut me out.

"We'd best get to the village," he said stiffly. "We dinna want to keep Marjorie and the lasses waitin'."

12

As they traveled the remaining distance to the village, Graeme cursed himself for being a thousand kinds of arse. He'd treated Berget like a common whore. Mayhap because he hadn't coupled with a respectable woman since his wife had killed herself.

He snorted in self-disgust, and she cast him a puzzled look.

Likely, she was completely confused by his hot and cold behavior, but he was struggling as much to understand himself as she, no doubt, was.

When he bedded a woman now, it was to satisfy a physical need no different than eating, drinking, or sleeping. In fact, he'd remained celibate for two years after Nairna's death. Until today, he'd told no one of the hateful things she'd hurled at him in the privacy of her bedchamber.

Things that emasculated and wounded his soul.

She'd convinced him no woman enjoyed sexual congress except for whores paid to do so.

It wasn't until after a rather personal and candid conversation with Sion that he learned the marriage bed could be delightful. At least his brother vowed it was so and that Marjorie enjoyed the act as much as he.

"Berget...?"

Those lavender eyes of hers, so innocent and unpretentious, met his. No judgment or condemnation glinted in their lovely depths. Only compassion and a hint of lingering arousal. "Yes?"

The heat of a flush crept over his face, and he checked the urge to clutch at his neckcloth. And shift in the saddle, for his manhood throbbed uncomfortably still. "I must beg yer forgiveness."

"Och, I dinna think so, Highlander." The alluring half-smile she gifted him held a siren's promise. "You'll not be apologizing for introducing me to passion. 'Tis been a gift I never thought to experience."

Shaking his head, he released a relieved chuckle. He'd never met a woman like her, and she was fast becoming far too important. "Lass, ye havena begun to experience passion with me."

She arched those fine brows of hers, a challenge slightly narrowing her eyes. "And what if I want you to teach me all that there is to know about carnal desire and lovemaking?" She captured her lower lip between her teeth, her gaze darting away for a second before she bravely brought it back to his. "I'm a widow without prospects. Should I never experience a man's touch?"

Introducin' me to passion. Never experience a man's touch?

What the hell?

He only now just realized what she'd said, and he sat a mite straighter as her previous words bludgeoned him with a cudgel's force. "What do ye mean *introducin'* ye to passion? Didna ye and yer husband never...? What I mean is—"

She held up her hand, her cheeks a fetching pink. "I know what you mean, and the answer is no. He couldn't. I suspect he was only able to perform with those poor boys he abused."

Disgust for Jonston and self-recrimination vied for supremacy behind Graeme's breastbone. He swore beneath his breath, not questioning her declaration of innocence, and that was all the more reason she was off limits.

"I don't suppose you'd be willing to teach me?" She crinkled her brow, turning down her mouth into a rueful frown. "But then, I could hardly stay on as a governess, could I?"

"Nae, lass. I dinna dally with those under my protection. As delectable as ye are and as much as I'd like to..." His gaze sank to her bountiful breasts her riding habit concealed before he hauled it upward, his molars clenched tight enough to crack his face. "I canna."

Damn him for a fool, but he didn't dare take what she innocently offered. Her virginity further complicated an already thorny situation. Even so, his cock throbbed unmercifully and called him every kind of idiot.

She didn't seem perturbed or offended by his denial. Surely, he ought to terminate her at once for her disgraceful suggestion. This wasn't the sort of woman he wanted his nieces spending hours a day with. *Was it?*

Her coy smile and the pointed look she directed to the tenting of his kilt sent sparks of scorching lust sluicing along his veins. She leaned forward, a hint of mischief in those gorgeous pansy-toned eyes. "Unless you plan on dismissing me, we'll be sleeping under the same roof every night. Think on that in your lonely bed."

As if he needed reminding.

"If I didn't need my position, I might actually consider seducing you," she murmured.

Christ and all the saints.

She gave him a cheeky grin and an even saucier wink.

He laughed then, unrestrained and delighted.

She'd done that on purpose, to take his mind off

Nairna. "Ye're the most unique, outrageous woman I've ever met."

Most remarkable and unforgettable too, and the thought of her ever leaving Killeaggian churned his stomach and left a hollowness he couldn't explain.

He hadn't quite brought his tumultuous emotions under control when they halted before The Stag and Hound. Swiftly perusing the area, he pulled his brows together, having expected Marjorie and the girls to be waiting nearby.

They weren't, however. Likely they were already seated inside.

A young boy collected the horses' reins, and Graeme slid to the ground to assist Berget. Several inquisitive villagers openly stared at the beautiful woman with their laird, and he lifted a hand as he nodded at them. "I hope we'll see ye at the *cèilidh*."

"Aye, Laird."

"We're lookin' forward to the celebration."

"Wouldna miss it, Laird."

"The villagers love and respect you too," she murmured beneath her breath, her gaze darting here and there as she took in the tidy township.

"Aye. I've always believed in treatin' others well and hope they'd do the same for me."

"I suppose."

He caught her troubled glance. Experience had taught them both that wasn't always the case. Tucking her hand into the crook of his elbow, he guided her inside. It took a moment for his eyes to adjust to the alehouse's darker interior.

Melvin Watson hurried to greet him, a pristine apron tied around his slim middle. His eyes widened upon taking in Berget on Graeme's arm. "My laird, what an honor it is to have ye dinin' with us this afternoon. Lady Marjorie and the wee lasses are already seated in the private parlor." He swept his hand to the side. "If ye'll follow me."

An amiable and relaxed hour passed. Graeme did, indeed, feel lighter for having shared with Berget about his failed marriage and the loss of his son.

She and Marjorie chatted like old friends, and Marjorie even conceded to implement a couple of Berget's suggestions for the celebration. On their best behavior, Cora and Elena dabbed their lips with their napkins, and only once did Cora use her fingers to pop a morsel of food into her mouth.

Not once did a finger up her nose precede a bite either.

Giving them a proud smile, he winked. "What have ye lasses done with my beloved nieces?" He pretended to search under the table. "Yer manners are much too refined to be those vixens. Confess what ye've done with them, or I'll toss ye in my dungeon. I'll have nae interlopers at my keep."

The girls erupted into giggles, but Berget darted him a distressed glance. Too late, he realized what his last words must sound like to her.

"The outdoors agrees with you, Miss Jonston," Marjorie suddenly said. "There's a healthy glow in your cheeks that wasn't there this morning."

"I've found the Highlands to be very ah...invigorating," Berget demurred, casting Graeme a covert glance.

Minx. Invigorating, his arse.

"Indeed," his sister-in-law remarked rather too smoothly.

He didn't miss the considering look Marjorie sent him.

Was she attempting to play matchmaker now?

He checked the upward bend of his mouth, though the notion didn't displease him as it once would have. However, things were complicated enough with Berget under his protection and also an employee.

And an untried maid.

There was the additional inconvenience that she was promised to someone else. He doubted that even if a settlement agreement had been signed by her father and Warrington, the claim would hold up in court. She was of age and couldn't be compelled to marry against her wishes unless by a royal decree.

He still needed to pen a letter to Camden, asking him to do a bit of poking about regarding Warrington and even Lord Stewart. What caused a nobleman to sell his daughter off to a debaucher? Twice? By God, Graeme would see to it that Berget never had to fear in that regard again.

As he spooned a bite of exceptional mutton stew into his mouth, he contemplated what Marjorie's reaction might be to the forged letters when he told her. She was a fair-minded person, gracious and forgiving. She wouldn't kick up a fuss about the references. He was sure of it.

Berget was good for the girls.

She was good for Marjorie.

And she was good for him. Very good.

So now, what precisely was he to do about her?

Did he dare trust himself to pursue a decent woman? He couldn't quite squelch the smile tilting his mouth at her early profession that she would seduce him. He'd rather like to see her try. Aye, that he would.

His humor faded and the bite of bread he swallowed lodged in his throat. No, he wouldn't. For he'd be honor bound to wed her, and that wasn't an option he was prepared to pursue.

13

Another week passed in a haze of activity.

The sheep shearing, lambing, and barley harvesting had taken place in the spring, but there were always a score of other duties to keep a laird busy day and night. Graeme directed the outdoor arrangements for the *cèilidh* while Marjorie had servants running hither and yon with her orders with other preparations for the celebration.

Berget continued her duties as governess, but there'd been no more mind-rattling kisses.

At times, he saw her watching him with a pensive expression.

Didn't she understand he'd nearly taken her beneath the trees? She'd be ruined if he yielded to his desires. Touching her would dissolve his barely controlled restraint, so he'd reverted to avoiding her again.

A short while later, one short rap preceded Camden sauntering into the study.

At once, Graeme rose and came around the desk to grip his brother's arm. "Welcome home."

"Ye look like hell." Grinning widely, Camden slapped Graeme's shoulder. "I'm surprised to see ye hidin' in here. That wouldna have anythin' to do with the new governess, would it?"

A hand clasped to his nape, Graeme sliced his brother a sharp look. "Ye've been talkin' to Marjorie already."

It wasn't a question.

Resting his hip on the edge of the desk, Camden folded his arms. "Is there anythin' to what she says?"

Quashing the urge to tell Camden to bugger himself, Graeme puffed out a long breath and turned to stare out the window. His brother meant well and only cared that he was happy. The same could be said for Marjorie.

In fact, truth be told, it astonished him how easily

she'd conceded to Berget.

"I've kissed the lass." He shot a glance over his shoulder. "More than once, in fact, and I told her about Nairna and Andrew too."

Camden released a low whistle and kicked his foot back and forth as he studied the carpet pattern. Finally, he lifted a shoulder. "So what's the problem then?"

"Besides that she's our nieces' governess?" Flicking up a finger, Graeme tapped it with the fingers of his other hand before raising two more. "That I promised her my protection and that means I canna take advantage of my position as laird? That she came here under false pretenses?"

"Dinna forget, she's bein' pursued by a lecherous bastard," Camden offered offhandedly.

"Och, there's that too." Graeme indicated the decanter on the sideboard. He wasn't revealing her virginity. That would remain a precious secret between her and him. "Care for a dram?"

Camden nodded as he fiddled with a letter opener, casually flipping it in the air and catching the hilt. "Aye. I'm fairly parched."

For a moment, the tinkling of crystal and the distinct gurgle of whisky splashing into tumblers were the only sounds in the vast room. Graeme strode across the floor and, after passing Camden his spirits, took a long swallow. He closed his eyes, bracing against the slow, welcome scorching to his belly.

"She really has ye tangled in knots, disna she, Brother?" No mocking accompanied the question.

Another sigh escaped Graeme. "Aye, because I believe I can really care for her. But after my first disastrous marriage...I dinna ken."

Camden cocked his head, the grin tugging at his mouth sympathetic rather than sarcastic.

"Since when have ye been afraid to fight for what ye want? Aye, yer first marriage was a disaster. Nae one is denyin' that, but that debacle wasna of yer makin'. Nairna would've been miserable with any mon. If ye and Berget have feelin's for each other, I think ye should pursue them."

As Graeme returned to his chair behind the desk, he waved the suggestion away. "Tell me what ye learned of Warrington and Stewart. Berget already confessed to forgin' the reference letters. Marjorie kens as well, and we're in agreement she only did so out of desperation. She's no' by nature a dishonest person."

Camden slid off the desk and, balancing his whisky tumbler, settled into a comfortable black leather wingback chair before propping his feet atop the desk and crossing his ankles.

Eyeing his brother's casual posture, Graeme arched an eyebrow, and Camden cocked his in return in a silent challenge.

"Warrington may no' be a buggering sod like Berget's first husband, but he has a licentious reputation. He's abusive to his servants, and from what I've been able to glean from speakin' to them, his wife fared nae better." He tipped back his tumbler, then grimaced. "The scunner frequents the profanest establishments in Edinburgh, and more than one whore has been severely injured, or worse, at his hands. He enjoys inflictin' pain."

"Christ." Graeme raked his hand through his hair. "There's nae question of her weddin' him, but I doubt he'll accept that. From what she's told me, he sounds obsessed with her. And I'll wager, he's an arrogant shite who thinks Berget ought to be grateful he'll have her."

With a sage nod, Camden shifted, crossing his other ankle atop the first.

"How much did he offer to pay Stewart for her?"

Graeme recalled how devastated she was to learn she'd been sold to her first husband for five thousand pounds.

Camden snorted, curling his lips in disgust. "A measly three thousand pounds."

"Seems the value he placed on his only child has decreased." Because he believed she was used goods? The bloody cur. "And that speaks of a mon with troubles spinnin' out of control."

"Aye, Stewart's a gambler, and he borrowed from disreputable cravens to keep up appearances," Camden agreed, leaning his head against the chair. "Some of the people he owes coin to have lost patience."

Scratching an eyebrow, Graeme sneered, "And I'll vow, he's already spent the money Warrington paid him, hasna he?" He sank back into his chair, shaking his head. "Do ye think he'd harm Stewart?"

His brother answered with a sharp nod. "Without a doubt to both questions. In the unsavory establishments I visited, rumors circulate about other people Warrington's loaned funds to. Many have ended up maimed or missin'."

Fingers steepled under his chin, Graeme leaned forward. "I gave my word to Berget that she could stay here as long as she desires, and I offered her a laird's protection." He shot a glance to the closed door. "Did ye discover who the other man was nosin' around the agency askin' questions about her?"

Tossing back the rest of his whisky, Camden nodded. Dropping his feet to the floor with a muffled thud, set the empty glass atop the desk. "'Twas Warrington. And what's more, I'm no' convinced the agency's owner, a Rupert Miller, didna accept a bribe from him."

Jerking his head up, Graeme slammed his palms flat onto the desktop. "Precisely what are ye implyin', Camden?"

"A clerk confessed—with a substantial monetary inducement from me—that he overheard a conversation. He believes Miller told Warrington where Berget is. I think the clerk was sweet on her. He admitted he sent her a warnin' letter, though he didna name me or Warrington."

"Shite!"

Fury and dread coursed through Graeme, and he pounded his fist atop the desk, rattling the inkpot. With a frustrated growl, he shoved to his feet. One hand cupping his chin and the other splayed on his hip, he paced back and forth.

"I did inquire at the inns I frequented on the way home if anyone of Warrington's description had been there. He's no' the sort of fellow ye can forget. No' with his stark white hair and black eyebrows. He has the look of the devil himself about him."

"And?" Was the bastard close?

A frustrated scowl contorted Camden's face. "He hadna been seen."

Whirling to face his brother, Graeme shook his head. "But there are dozens of other inns he might've stopped at if he's journeyin' here."

Graeme swore again. "Dammit."

"So, what are we goin' to do, Brother?" Camden asked.

Head lifted and eyes narrowed, Graeme stared hard at the door.

He had no choice. This was the best course to ensure Berget's safety.

"There's only one way I can truly protect Berget now." He slanted a resigned glance to Camden. "Ride at once to the village and return with the priest."

14

Berget hummed as she strolled the lawns with Cora and Elena. Despite her best efforts, the girls had removed their bonnets and were currently intent on catching a butterfly.

Evidently, butterflies were rare this far north, and the girls were ecstatic to see the coppery-orange and inky-black creature flitting about.

A soft smile arced her mouth. She loved it here.

She'd found a peace she hadn't expected at Killeaggian Tower. Aside from Graeme's retreat behind the wall he'd erected between them, she was content. The tiny ember of hope that the attraction between them might grow into something more had all but died.

It had only been in the last couple of days she

recognized the sorrow squeezing her heart for what it truly was. She'd done the rashest thing and fallen in love with him.

A rider thundered down the lane from the keep's entrance, and she shaded her eyes against the sun, squinting to make out who he was.

Her breath left her lungs in a whoosh upon recognizing Camden.

When had he returned?

And why was he leaving again already?

A chill skittered along her spine, and she shivered. She'd confessed everything to Graeme, and he'd shared the details with Lady Marjorie. Berget kept no more secrets, except for her love for him. Nevertheless, uneasiness prickled down her spine again.

In the short while since she'd come to live here, she'd come to love the people and the land. She could easily see herself spending the remainder of her days in the Highlands. But the girls would only need a governess for a decade at most.

Then what was to become of her?

What was more, could she bear abiding ten years

under the roof with a man she adored, never having her love requited? Berget didn't have an answer for that. Would it be worse to remain or leave and possibly never see him again?

She didn't miss her parents either. That made her a horrible daughter or a person who'd experienced enough manipulation in her lifetime and had determined to forge her own future from now on.

"Cora, Elena, let's return to the keep." She extended her hands, and after a few halfhearted cries of disappointment, the girls scampered to her sides and clasped her fingers.

"I still dinna understand how a butterfly comes from a poop," Cora said, her small forehead furrowed in confusion.

"Pupa," Elena corrected, glancing to Berget for confirmation.

"Yes, butterflies form pupas or a chrysalis, and moths spin a silken cocoon," Berget affirmed.

"I wish we could see one borned," Elena sighed.

Berget didn't correct her and explain they weren't born but underwent metamorphosis.

"I wish you could too. But honestly, I don't even know where to look for pupas or cocoons in the Highlands. Let me conduct a bit of research in the library and see if I can discover the plants they prefer. Perhaps we might come upon one if we're very lucky."

As they sauntered up the sloping hill, she smiled at a pair of calves butting heads in a neighboring field. They were an unusual breed with thick, wavy black hair, and unlike anything she'd ever seen in the Lowlands. A few Highland cows also mingled with the Galloways.

As she and the girls neared the top of the lawn, Lady Marjorie descended a stone staircase leading to a cozy enclosed courtyard at the rear of the castle. Wearing the same saffron-colored gown she'd worn when Berget first met her, today she'd plaited her hair and wound it around her head. She truly was a lovely woman.

She met them at the corbeled arched entrance, a smile on her lips but a tinge of tension crimping the edges of her eyes.

"My darlings," she said, bending to kiss each

daughter atop her head. "Maive has just taken pear tarts from the oven. She specifically asked me to find you so that you may test her new recipe." She angled her head and tapped her chin with her forefinger, seemingly undecided. "That is, if you can be persuaded to come indoors."

The girls needed no further urging before they clasped hands and scampered off.

"Make sure you wash your face and hands first," their mother called. Shaking her head, she bent her mouth into a wry smile. "Do you supposed they'll do as I bid?"

Berget knew her charges well enough by now to know they wouldn't.

"No." She dangled their discarded bonnets. "I'm still working on convincing them of the necessity of wearing a bonnet to protect their skin. I'm sure Cook won't let them touch a tart until they are well scrubbed though."

Lady Marjorie looped her arm through Berget's, and her earlier uneasiness returned.

"Is aught the matter?" she asked.

Marjorie sighed, and, taking Berget's hands in hers, gave her fingers a little squeeze. "Graeme wishes to speak with you at once."

Berget drew her eyebrows together and turned her mouth downward into a small, confused frown. "Is something amiss? Have I done something wrong?"

That fear always niggled at the back of her mind. Even though Lady Marjorie, Graeme, and everyone else of the keep had been nothing but gracious to her.

"Berget, may I ask you something personal?" Usually straightforward, there was an unusual hesitancy in Lady Marjorie's question.

Searching her new friend's face, Berget couldn't fathom her poignant expression. "Of course. I'll answer if I can."

Marjorie steered her gaze over Berget's shoulder for a moment before bringing it back and offering one of her genial smiles. "Are you happy here?"

That was what she wanted to ask her? Berget would've sworn it was something much more profound or worrisome.

"I am." She allowed a small smile. "Far more

content than I'd ever expected. In fact, more so than I've been for most of my life."

Chagrin chafed her conscience again.

Initially, she'd believed herself unrepentant for forging the documents, but the truth of it was as soon as she'd arrived at Killeaggian Tower and met Graeme and Marjorie, remorse had pummeled her. "I know I used false measures to obtain the position, but I thought…"

"Don't fret about that." Shaking her head fervently, Marjorie clasped Berget's hands firmly. "That's not why I asked, anyway. Do you care for Graeme?"

The direct question so took Berget back, her jaw slackened for an instant. "He's the laird. I'm a governess. It would be most unseemly of me to direct my regard toward him."

Oh God, she's learned of the kisses somehow. And now I'll lose my position.

A fragile smile tipped Lady Marjorie's mouth. "I'd hoped you harbored stronger emotions for him. He's a man deserving of love."

Why would she say that?

Berget had no idea how to respond, for what she'd said was true. A governess had no business entertaining romantic notions toward her employer. Particularly the keep's laird who'd become distant and reserved since their last kiss.

Which told her unequivocally that he harbored no interest in pursuing a relationship with her.

She'd only been half-jesting about seducing him. Naturally, she had no idea how to go about such a thing. Besides, did she really want to ruin her reputation?

With Graeme, it might've been worth it.

While it had been fun to flirt, she knew as well as he that things could go no further. She'd learn to bear the pain of her secret love. In time.

Before Berget could respond to Marjorie's last comment, the object of their discussion descended the stairs. Graeme's vivid blue gaze flicked between them, and his well-formed mouth tightened the merest bit.

"Marjorie, would you give me a few moments with Berget, please?"

She nodded. "Of course." As she moved to pass them, she paused and touched his forearm. "Are you positive you wish to do this?"

Do what?

Terminate Berget's employment?

Emotion and panic surged up her chest, but she sternly tamped them down. She'd face her dismissal with poise and grace. He'd never hear her heart shattering or see the distress in her expression.

He gave a terse nod. "I am. 'Tis the only way."

Her heart sank further still. Swallowing, her teeth clamped tight, she clenched her fingers together, willing herself to be brave and not to weep.

Sending her a compassionate glance, Lady Marjorie gave the smallest nod before turning and ascending the stairs.

Graeme said not a word until she disappeared into the arched stone entry atop the landing. Then he extended his arm, his eyes hooded and expression unreadable. "Walk with me."

"Graeme, if you're going to discharge me, I'd prefer you did so straightaway."

His brows flew high on his forehead, his eyes flexing the merest bit. "Whatever gave ye the idea that I intended to dismiss ye?"

Her gaze veered to the empty portico, then gravitated back to him.

"I thought...Lady Marjorie said..." She moistened her lips and, though trepidation's sharp claws scraped across her shoulders, she noticed his focus slide to her mouth for an instant. "Perhaps I misunderstood. What did you wish to say to me?"

"Camden's returned, and the information he's brought is verra disturbin'." He took her elbow and led her to a stone bench situated along one side of the courtyard beneath a tree's overhanging branches. After urging her to sit, he settled beside her and gathered her hand in his.

She stared at their entwined fingers. Why had he let his guard down now? What was the nature of the news that had caused this abrupt change in his behavior?

"How so?" she asked. "I've told you everything. I swear, I have."

"He's discovered that Warrington is the other man inquirin' after ye, and Camden believes he bribed or coerced the agency owner into revealin' yer location."

"No!" Berget gasped, clasping her other hand to her breast. Her heart raced, and her stomach tumbled over itself sickeningly.

"I'm afraid so, lass. Even now, we believe he journeys here."

"Why won't that devil's spawn leave me be?" she cried.

With his other hand, Graeme caressed the top of hers.

"Yer father's already spent the money Warrington gave him as part of the marriage settlement. And given the unsavory things Camden uncovered about Warrington, I believe only one way remains to truly protect ye. Other than runnin' him through, which I'd no' hesitate to do if I must. The mon's an absolute reprobate, and I'll no' allow him near ye."

"So you're sending me away."

15

"I understand." Blinking back stinging tears, Berget forced the words from her mouth. "He poses a danger to Marjorie and the girls. To your clan and perhaps the villagers too. Especially if he is as evil as you say."

And Warrington was. Probably worse than anything she might imagine.

A rough sound rumbled deep in Graeme's throat.

"I should go pack at once." She tried to withdraw her hand, but he tightened his grip.

Grazing his knuckles across her cheek, a tender smile tilted his mouth. "Ye're always willin' to think ye're at fault and to sacrifice yerself. I didna mean ye're to leave, *leannan*. What I'm suggestin' is that we must marry straightaway. I've sent Camden to the village for Father Phillip."

That was why he'd thundered away like hell's hounds pursued him.

Berget gaped as his words took root, and a little tremor of excitement and hope jolted through her. "You would marry me? After...everything?"

He ran his thumb over her lips, "Aye, my violet-eyed lass, I would gladly marry ye."

"Are you absolutely certain, Graeme?" She examined every angle and plane of his dear face, striving to determine his sincerity. "Marriage is for a lifetime. I know you didn't intend to wed again, and as much as I want to say yes, if your only motivation is to protect me from Warrington, then I must refuse."

He stiffened, going perfectly still except for the merest quivering of his nostrils. Had he truly thought she'd agree out of a selfish desire for his protection?

His intense scrutiny never leaving her, he spoke slowly and deliberately. "I made a vow to ye, lass, that ye would be safe here. And as I told ye before, I keep my oaths. This is the only way I can protect ye."

"I know, because you're an honorable man. But

you've already entered into a marriage once before that you didn't want, and you were utterly miserable as a consequence." She inhaled, forcing her lips upward though her heart fractured further with each word she spoke. "I cannot let you do that again. Even though your motives are pure and unselfish, and I'm grateful you're willing to make such a magnanimous sacrifice for me."

Neither could she wed him if he didn't love her. What happened if the day came and he met a woman he could love, but he was tied to her?

No. She wouldn't do that to him.

She made to stand, desperately trying to stem the flood of tears that threatened. "Now excuse me, please. I must pack." The task would take all of ten minutes. She'd brought so little with her.

But instead of releasing her, he pulled her onto his lap and framed her face with his big hands. "Och, woman. Ye'll drive me mad. Ye'd have me tell ye what I havena even admitted to myself."

"Tell me what," she sniffled, disgusted at her display of tears.

He kissed her forehead then the tip of her nose. "I would make ye mine, no' out of duty or honor or responsibility. I would protect ye, Berget, because ye've come to mean more to me than mortal words can say. The thought of ye leavin' the keep—leavin' *me*—is unbearable."

She went perfectly immobile, afraid to blink or to breathe. She searched his eyes, seeing her own wonder and awe reflected there.

"Graeme...are ye sayin' ye *care* for me?"

Hope flared, a minuscule spark, but that minute ember was enough to encourage her.

His gaze grew dark, intense, almost predatory, and a possessive gleam glimmered there. "I canna let ye leave, *mo ghaol*."

His love. Could it be true?

"I canna bear no' seein' ye every day. Yer smile, the way yer lavender eyes light up at the smallest things. The tender way ye treat the lasses, and the kindness ye show everyone. My heart swells, causin' a fierce ache whenever ye nuzzle the pups or kiss their downy heads. Or when I hear yer laugh, yer singin', or when ye play the lute or harp. My food tastes better when we dine at the same table. The sun glows brighter, and the sky's more vivid blue with ye by my side."

That sounded very much like a man in love, and her pulse and breathing quickened.

He settled his lips atop hers, kissing her once. Twice. Three times. His mouth firm and warm and tasting of whisky.

"I've fallen in love with ye, Berget."

With a cry of joy, she looped her arms around his neck. "Oh, Graeme. I dared not hope. I tried to fight my feelings. I so wanted you to admire me and respect me and not think ill of me after I said I would seduce you." Her face burned at that admission. "You made me feel things that I never felt before and, with you, I was daring and bold and wanton."

He arced a wicked brow, giving her a devilish smile.

"Och, lass, I mean to hold ye to that promise to seduce me." Trailing a finger along the edge of her bodice, he rasped in her ear, "So, will ye marry me as soon as my brother returns with the priest? It will no' be a fancy weddin'. Just ye, me, Camden, Marjorie, and the lasses."

She didn't care about all the folderol. She only wanted to be his. "Aye, I shall very happily marry you."

He gave a little growl and captured her mouth with his, and she reveled in his embrace. He cradled one breast, teasing the nipple through her gown's fabric and beneath her bum, his length swelled, hard and powerful.

This glorious man loved her.

She never dreamed it possible. That she could love someone so profoundly, so deeply, that his very spirit meshed with hers. That she desired to give herself to him in every way possible. She hungered for his touch with a ravenous craving she wouldn't have believed if she hadn't experienced it firsthand.

"Graeme! Berget!" Marjorie's urgent summons doused Berget's ardor.

With an embarrassed flush scorching her from waist to forehead, she scrambled off Graeme's lap and promptly set to righting her rumpled clothing.

He gazed up at his sister-in-law hanging over the balustrade, her face pale and troubled. "Marjorie, yer timin' is awful, but I'm honored to say Berget has consented to be my wife."

Berget cast him a shy smile as she finished straightening her gown and moved to setting her hair in order.

"Never mind that." Marjorie scowled and gestured for them to come quickly. "That dreadful man is *here*. Barged right into the house without an invitation or a by your leave. He gives me the shivers, I tell you."

In the process of repinning a loose tendril of hair, Berget fumbled, her fingers gone suddenly stiff.

No' Warrington. Please dinna let it be Warrington.

But even as she sent the frantic prayer skyward, he appeared beside Marjorie on the landing, still wearing his hat and, oddly enough, an elaborate cloak, despite the mild weather.

He was every bit as disturbing and unsettling as she remembered.

Marjorie speared him a contemptuous glare. "You were instructed to wait in the drawing room, sir, and instead, you dared to follow me?"

"Indeed, I did." His lewd gaze undressed her before he gave a dismissive sniff. "I wasn't providing you the opportunity to warn my bride so that she could flee me once more. I've spent weeks searching for her."

Berget could scarcely pull air into her lungs. The man had no compunction. To breeze into the keep uninvited and then to follow Marjorie. Did he have no scruples?

A smug, closed-mouth smile tipping his thin lips upward a fraction, his coal-black eyes swung between Berget and Graeme.

"Laird Kennedy, I presume," he intoned with frigid contempt.

Graeme curled his lip in response.

Warrington turned his wintery gaze upon Berget, and goosebumps raised from her wrists to her shoulders. He radiated evilness. "Please do explain why I find you disheveled and in the company of this man, *Wife*."

Jerking as if slapped, Berget snapped her head up, and her mouth parted on an astonished gasp. Husbanding every ounce of poise she possessed, she returned his condescending stare straight on. "I am not your wife, nor shall I ever be."

He smiled widely then, an eerie upward sweep of his too-thin lips. The remainder of his face remained steely and unyielding.

"But, my dear, this document says otherwise." Brandishing a folded paper, he leaned casually against the balustrade. "'Tis a proxy marriage contract, you see. And it most assuredly deems *we are* married." His focus trailed to her breasts, then lower still before he licked those pale lips. "Except for the consummation, which will occur just as soon as I remove you from the premises."

She wouldn't put it past him to set upon her in the coach.

"Over my dead body." Graeme surged to his feet, a dangerous growl reverberating deep in his chest. "There nae be proxy marriages in Scotland. Irregular marriages, aye, but no' proxies. That bit of paper is nae more valuable than what I wipe my arse with."

"Ah, but this proxy marriage wasn't acquired in Scotland." Warrington waved the rolled document. "'Twas authorized in England and is legally binding there," he gloated. "My many high-level connections made it possible."

High level, indeed.

Likely he'd threatened some poor sot to draft the document or bribed an official or cleric to do so. How he acquired the proxy was irrelevant. What did matter was whether it was valid.

Berget clutched Graeme's hand. She had no knowledge of such things, and terror worse than any she'd experienced pulsed unrelentingly through her, making her dizzy.

"Graeme, could he be telling the truth?"

He couldn't. *Oh, god, he couldn't.* It must be a lie. The desperate attempt of a madman. His obsession with her had crossed into lunacy.

A fierce scowl hardened Graeme's face to granite. "I dinna think so, lass. I'm nae expert on proxy marriages, but they usually only take place between royalty, when one party is in another country. Then when they are on the same soil, an official ceremony is performed before any consummation occurs."

"What are we to do?" She swallowed, edging nearer and fighting the fear clawing at her throat.

"Dinna fash yerself." He possessively looped an arm about her waist, clearly staking his claim. 'Ye ken I'll nae let him take ye from here as long as I have breath in my lungs."

Warrington narrowed his eyes to lethal slits.

"I'm warning you, Kennedy. Unhand my wife. We are leaving. Now. Berget, you belong to me. I paid the price your pathetic father asked, and the wretch already spent the funds. There is no denying my claim."

"You made an arrangement with my father that I never agreed to. More fool you for doing so, since you well knew his character and his weaknesses. I shall never willingly leave with you," Berget vowed. "And I shall never consent to becoming your wife. You cannot force me."

More commotion echoed behind Marjorie and Warrington as Camden and a kindly-faced, reed-thin priest joined them on the landing.

Marjorie elbowed Warrington hard in the ribs before seizing the priest's hand. Practically dragging the startled clergyman down the stairs, she whispered in his ear all the while. He nodded and cast a harried glance over his shoulder, his tunic flapping against his legs in his hasty descent.

"What are you doing?" Suspicion contorting his countenance, Warrington lunged toward the stairs.

Marjorie swung around, pointing at him, and shouted, "Camden, keep that cur there."

"I don't think so." With a sharp gesture, Warrington yanked a flintlock from the folds of his cloak.

At once, Camden looped his massive arm around Warrington's neck, and pulled the man's arm behind his back, forcing the limb so unnaturally high that Warrington blanched and swore but dropped the weapon. He continued to struggle, and Camden tightened his grip.

"Give me a reason to snap yer arm or yer neck," Camden sneered, low and dangerous. "Because I have nae qualms about doin' either and confessin' my sin to Father Phillip afterward."

Father Phillip mopped his moist forehead, then folded his hands serenely before him. "I believe an abbreviated version of the weddin' ceremony would be most appropriate."

"I forbid it," Warrington roared. "I'm her husband."

Camden flexed his jaw and yanked Warrington's arm, producing a furious howl of pain.

Uneasiness flitted across Father Phillip's angular face. "I must ask ye, lass, does he speak the truth? I shall no' be a party to bigamy."

"No." Berget vehemently shook her head. "I have never exchanged vows with that man, and I never will. I am unwed."

"He claims to have a proxy contract executed in England," Graeme explained.

"Does he now?" Father Phillip winked before casting a dismissive glance over his shoulder to where Camden held Warrington in a punishing embrace.

Berget liked the cleric at once.

"I think it is safe to assume 'tis forged," Father Phillip said, his eyes twinkling as if he were enjoying this fiasco. "I ken of nae instances of commoners joinin' by proxy, but just in case it isna a counterfeit, lass, ye'll want to stay in Scotland."

She turned an adoring glance on Graeme. "For the rest of my life."

Warrington continued to curse and threaten.

At some point, Peigi and another wide-eyed maid appeared on either side of Camden.

Good, the more witnesses, the better. The next thing Berget knew, Peigi's bobcap had been stuffed inside Warrington's mouth, and the chipper little maid wore an extremely pleased expression.

Berget was of a mind to promote her to her lady's maid. "Do carry on, Father Phillip," she said, waving her hand.

In short order, Berget and Graeme exchanged vows in what was quite likely the swiftest and most abbreviated wedding ceremony in the history of Scotland. With another mischievous grin, Father Phillip announced, "I now pronounce ye man and wife. Ye may kiss yer bride, Laird."

16

Four hours later, after Camden and three other clansmen had escorted Warrington from Killeaggian Tower lands with threats to do him bodily harm if he ever returned, and after explaining to an overjoyed Cora and Elena that Berget had become their aunt, and Graeme had announced to the staff that Berget was now mistress of the keep, Berget entered her chamber.

Butterfly wings whisked around her middle about what the evening would bring. A mere fortnight ago, she'd entered this pleasant room for the first time, uncertain if she'd be permitted to stay.

Now she was married to the laird. Her heart surged with uncontrollable joy.

A bath waited for her before the hearth where a

roaring fire blazed. Several vases of colorful flowers had been placed about the chamber, and pale pink petals lay sprinkled atop the turned-down bed. A bottle of wine and two glasses sat prominently on the table beside a covered tray Berget had yet to explore but which likely contained dainties and other tasty morsels.

Graeme was *always* hungry.

Marjorie's doing, no doubt.

Instead of becoming jealous or shrewish that Berget had won Graeme's affection, Marjorie seemed genuinely happy for them and had gone out of her way to be kind.

A light rap echoed on Berget's door, and her attention flashed to the bedside clock. Was Graeme that eager to bed her? Scarcely fifteen minutes had passed since she'd left the great hall.

"Come," she called, though her new husband would have to wait until she'd enjoyed her bath. Maidenly shyness aside, she wanted to be at her best when she laid with him.

Marjorie glided into the room, a delicate night rail

slung over one slender arm. She smiled in approval as she glanced about the chamber. "Ah, good. The maids have done as I asked. Here, I brought you this." She extended the filmy fabric, thin as gossamer. "There wasn't any time to purchase you a proper gift, given how rushed everything was. But this will do for tonight, until I decide on something more appropriate and long-lasting for you and Graeme."

Accepting the beautiful nightgown, Berget's eyes blurred with tears. "Thank you. I owe you much."

Marjorie enveloped her in a warm hug. "You've made Graeme happy, and I've already come to think of you as a sister. I knew the minute I saw the two of you together in the drawing room something sparked betwixt you." Her expression turned melancholy as she fingered the ring on her hand. "He reminds me so much of Sion. I cannot bear to look at him sometimes."

That last statement said what Marjorie couldn't.

She missed her husband so much that she'd sought to ease her grief with the brother who bore such a striking resemblance to him. What Marjorie needed was another man to engage her affections. Not to make her forget her husband but to help her create new memories. Berget wasn't sure that was possible when one had loved so deeply though.

"He's made me very happy too," Berget admitted. And to think she'd considered him an uncouth barbarian that first morning. Yes, but he was her untamed Highlander, and she wouldn't have him any other way.

"I am miffed that I shall have to find another governess, however," Marjorie complained. But the twinkle in her eye belied any real disapproval. "As you know, they aren't easy to come by, and I cannot bear to send the girls away to school."

"I'd be happy to continue until another is retained." Berget draped the nightgown over the end of the bed. "I've enjoyed teaching the girls."

"Here, let me help you with your laces. Turn around," Marjorie directed. "I appreciate the offer, but you'll be much too busy overseeing the keep. There's much to learn. I'll help you, of course. But as the laird's wife, you'll have many obligations." She paused in her ministrations. "I don't suppose you could recommend a replacement?"

At once, Emeline came to mind. Would her friend consider such a thing to escape her domineering aunt?

"I might know someone. Let me write and ask her if she's interested. In fact, if you've no objection, I can invite her to the celebration. Then you can meet her yourself."

Emeline would assuredly enjoy a reprieve from her starchy aunt, and she'd also have a chance to visit with Arieen Wallace.

"That would be wonderful." Marjorie patted Berget's shoulder. "There, I think you can manage the rest yourself. Now, hurry and take your bath. Graeme was eyeing the hall entrance but seconds after you departed."

With a little laugh and a wave, she swept from the bedchamber.

Once Berget had divested herself of her garments, she sank into the lavender and rose-scented bath. Sighing as the fragrant water lapped over her, she leaned her head against the tub's rim. She lifted her hand, angling it this way and that, allowing the candlelight to catch the amethyst encircled by diamonds ring Graeme had slipped on her finger before they'd dined.

"It matches yer eyes, *leannan*. There's a matchin' necklace and earring' too."

Giddiness frolicked in her middle and not a little apprehension about what tonight would bring. She was married again, but this time to a man whose very glance heated her blood and made her ache for want of him.

Heeding Marjorie's warning, she quickly lathered a sponge and soaped herself. She'd just finished rinsing a leg, holding it above the water, when the door whisked open.

"Och, now that's a wondrous sight I'll no' soon forget."

The huskiness in Graeme's voice set her stomach to quivering, and with a little self-conscience squeak, she sank low in the water.

Hair damp and face freshly shaven, he chuckled as he stalked toward the tub, wearing only an unlaced shirt and a kilt slung low on his lean hips. He loomed above her, the cooling bath providing no protection from his probing stare. His avid gaze swept over the outline of her nipples before gravitating to the shadowy triangle at the juncture of her thighs.

He snatched the fluffy linen from the stool beside the tub and snapped it open. "Come, Wife."

Forcing her nervousness into submission, Berget rose to stand proudly before him.

"Perfection," he breathed huskily, skimming a finger across the swell of one breast. "I imagined ye naked, but ye're far more exquisite than I dreamed."

She trembled but not from fear, and desire darkened his eyes to cobalt.

Making a rough, animalistic noise in his throat, he swept her into his arms, and in five long strides of his muscular thighs, he reached the bed. He tenderly laid her atop the mattress before unwrapping the linen and staring his fill.

"Not fair. You're still dressed," she said, as much to cover her nervousness as because she needed to see him naked too.

"Never say I displeased ye, my lady love." With

deft movements, he shucked his shirt over his head, revealing a startling wide chest covered with that same reddish-blond hair. Sculpted muscles rippled across his torso, and a pulse ticked a wild rhythm in his corded neck.

His hand at his waist, he hesitated for an instant.

She raised up on one elbow and cocked a brow, deliberately thrusting her breasts upward. "Bashful, are ye, my Highland scoundrel?"

With a growl, he swept the plaid from his narrow hips. His engorged manhood jutted upward toward his flat belly from a thatch of darker blond hair, and she swallowed, a bit of her bravado dissolving

Dear God, he was magnificent. Sculpted male perfection. And he was her husband. *Her husband.*

He placed one knee on the bed, feathering his hands across her shoulders before pulling the pins from her hair and spreading the tresses. "Are ye afraid, lass?"

Berget slid her hands over his chest, then brazenly encircled his engorged length. "Nae. I'm a seductress, remember? Now make me yours for now and all time, Graeme."

He came to her then, playing her body like a finely tuned instrument, and when she could stand it no longer, when she'd ceased thinking coherently, he slid into her.

She cried out and dug her fingers into his back, her breath coming in short pants.

"Easy, *mo ghoal*. Relax and let yer body become accustomed to me inside ye," he whispered into her ear, one hand cradling her hip and the other fondling her breast. He murmured words of love and sex, his hands caressing and soothing.

After a few moments, the pain eased and she became aware of his fullness stretching her. She tentatively moved her pelvis, gasping as delicious sensation spiraled from her core outward.

Graeme rocked his hips, and another burst of bliss swept her.

"Oh, Graeme," she breathed, arching into him as he slowly plunged and withdrew. "'Tis...wonderful."

"Aye, and this is only the beginnin'."

He quickened his pace, and Berget met him stroke for stroke, the movements sending her higher and higher. Sensation so powerful she wasn't sure she could take anymore burned through her veins like a wildfire, engulfing and uncontrollable, until she reached a pinnacle. And then she was falling, shattering, crying out his name over and over as blissful ecstasy convulsed through her in wave after devastating wave.

Graeme slid his hands beneath her hips, raising them higher as he surged deeper still. With a guttural groan, he stiffened before collapsing atop her. Several minutes passed, her limbs leaden and her breathing ragged beneath his welcoming weight.

He rolled off her, tucking her into his side and pressing a long kiss to her temple. "I never kent it could be like that."

She touched her mouth to his chest. "I love you."

"And I love ye, my jewel-eyed lass." He drew lazy circles on her bare hip. "I dinna ken what our future holds, *leannan*, and I fear Scotland's future as well, but with ye by my side, I can face anythin'."

Smiling seductively, she slid atop him, a thrill jolting through her at his strangled moan. "Can we do it again with me on top this time?"

He cupped her bottom, tilting his pelvis into hers. "Aye, and many other ways too."

"Will you show me all of them?" she purred, spreading her thighs and settling onto his hips.

"I'll spend a lifetime lovin' ye, lass."

"And I ye."

Epilogue

August 1720
Cèilidh Celebration
Killeaggian Tower

All the preparations for the *cèilidh* were complete and, at last, the week-long celebration was upon Killeaggian Tower. For the past three days, the keep had hummed with the arrival of guest after guest and the surrounding lands reverberated with the thumps, clanks, and banging which accompanied the pitching of tents and pavilions.

At last count, four and sixty—not counting servants—occupied the bedchambers, and dozens more clansmen bunked in the barracks or stables. Berget had no idea how many people occupied the tents, nor how many villagers mingled outside.

She clasped Emeline and Arieen's hands. "I'm so happy you could come. I've missed you terribly!"

Aireen grinned and hugged her. "Who would've guessed that when we last saw each other at the McCullough's ball that we'd both be wed the next time we met?" She looped her elbow with Emeline's. "Now we must find *you* a husband."

Emeline blanched, swiftly casting a troubled glance around the hall. "Aunt Jeneva has her own ideas about that, I fear. She's been hintin' her third cousin would make an estimable husband." She grimaced and wrinkled her nose.

"Hmph. You aren't married yet, and there are scores of eligible men swarming the place for the next week," Berget declared. "In fact, I vow I saw more than one man eyeing you with appreciation during dinner last night. And remember, the position as governess is available if you are interested."

A rosy flush blooming across her cheeks, Emeline shushed her. "Shh. Aunt will drag me home straightaway if she hears ye. I canna quite believe she accompanied me. I did insist I meant to attend with or without her permission. That sent her into a peevish sulk, but she kens I'm of age, and she truly has no control over me. I do have a mind of my own, ye ken."

Just then, a laughing Marjorie entered with Kendra MacKay and Bethea and Branwen Glanville. Keane, the Duke of Roxdale and cousin to Graeme, had come after all, arriving yestereve. His late father had been Bethea and Branwen's godfather, and after his father's death, he'd become the sisters' guardian.

Marjorie smiled broadly and made short work of introducing the women to Arieen and Emeline. She was fast becoming the sister Berget had never had.

"We've met before, Emeline. At McCullough's ball." Kendra chuckled, tossing her unbound chestnut hair over her shoulder. "I was dressed as a shieldmaiden."

"I remember." Emeline offered a shy smile. "Yer costume was brilliant."

Eyes alight with mischief, Kendra grinned. "I thought so too, but my brother wouldna agree." She puffed out her chest and lowered her voice. "Kendra

Mackay. Ye look like a strumpet."

The women all laughed.

"Keane never permits us to attend balls or visit Edinburgh or Inverness." Branwen caught her sister's eye. They were so similar in appearance they might be mistaken for twins, except she was slightly taller with midnight black hair while her sister's hair was a deep, warm sable. Both had pewter-grey eyes that gleamed with keen intelligence.

Bethea nodded as she swept her gaze around the hall. "But at least he finally agreed to attend the *cèilidh*. It took days of cajolin', and I think he only agreed to hush us."

"Berget, Graeme is looking for you," Marjorie said with an impish grin. "He and several of the other men are performing the sword dance."

Even before she finished speaking, the piper's music carried inside the keep. Berget marched swiftly through the entry and gatehouse. The outer gate stood wide open, and hundreds of people milled about.

With Arieen and Emeline at her side, they hurried toward the bagpipes' music. A large crowd had gathered, and smiling and excusing herself, she wended her way through the guests. Four pipers formed a neat row as they warmed up, and across from them eight kilted men stood at the ready, two swords crossed before each of the brawny Highlanders.

Arieen clasped Berget's arm. "Do ye see the look Keane, the Duke of Roxdale, is givin' Laird Kennedy?"

"Yes." The duke's raven brows nearly touched as he glowered at Graeme. "There's an unpleasant history between their families, though they are cousins."

Every bit the warrior that Graeme was, at first glance, the slightly older duke didn't resemble his cousin at all. Upon closer inspection, however, Graeme and Roxdale had the same chiseled jaw and hawkish brows. Their builds were similar as well. Marjorie claimed they'd rarely spent time in each other's company, and she'd frankly been surprised when Roxdale had accepted the invitation.

Graeme winked and bent into a gallant bow. Cora and Elena jumped up and down beside Camden and clapped their hands. "Uncle Graeme. Uncle Graeme."

The pipers began playing in earnest and, at once, the men launched into the dance steps.

That such large men could move with such agility and grace amazed Berget. It soon became clear the dance was a competition between Graeme and Roxdale. The music went on and on, and one by one the other men dropped out until only Graeme and his cousin continued to dance.

Originally, the sword dance had been a war dance, and clearly a battle commenced between the cousins and neither appeared willing to cede. Better this than fists or swords. Sweat beaded their foreheads and dripped from their temples, and their breathing came in harsh rasps.

It was the pipers who finally quit, declaring a drastic and immediate need for ale.

Grinning, Graeme swiped his forehead with the back of his hand and extended his other arm. "Well done, Cousin."

For a lengthy, tense moment, Roxdale stared, unmoving, at Graeme's arm. His mouth suddenly twitched into a smile and Berget blinked at the transformation in his features. He was...*beautiful*. He clasped Graeme's forearm soundly. "Now, where can a mon get a dram?"

Camden clapped him on the back. "I'll show ye, just as soon as I find the lasses' mother."

"I'm right here." Marjorie sailed into view and gave Roxdale an indiscernible glance before claiming her daughters' hands.

"I believe ye've met my brother's widow." Graeme swiped the sweat from his brow again. "The bonnie wee lasses are Cora and Elena."

To Berget's delight, the girls bobbed perfect curtsies, murmuring, "Your Grace."

Marjorie fairly beamed. "Come, my darlings, 'tis time for you to eat."

"I'm hungry myself, Lady Marjorie." Roxdale shoved his raven mane behind his shoulders. "May I join ye and the lasses?"

A startled look fluttered across her face before she pinkened and nodded. "Of course."

Hands on his hips, Camden shook his head. "I never thought I'd see the day a mon would turn down a dram to dine with wee lassies."

"Hold yer wheesht, Brother." Graeme gave him a

friendly warning. "Why do ye ken I let her invite him?"

Camden stared after them. "Ah, so that's how it is. Now ye're playin' Cupid." He winked wickedly. "See what ye've done to my brother, Berget? The next thing ye ken, he'll decide I need to wed."

Graeme drew Berget to his side, kissing her temple. "Wedded life isna so awful. Ye should consider—"

Throwing his hands up as if warding off evil spirits, Camden shook his head and backed away. "Nae. Dinna get any ideas. I have nae intention of marryin' for years and *years*."

He turned on his heel and disappeared into the crowd.

"I need to freshen up, *jo*." Graeme gave her a boyish grin. "I may have been showin' off a wee bit."

She raised a brow but held her tongue. Did men never outgrow the need to show off?

Five minutes later, she poured water from a pitcher onto a cloth as he stripped his damp shirt off over his broad shoulders. As always, when seeing his muscular form, her insides tumbled over. She passed him the wet cloth, and he briskly rubbed his face and neck, then wiped his chest and torso.

She kicked her shoes off, then crawled onto their immense bed. "Must you return to our guests straightaway?"

He slowly turned, a predator's smile upon his face. "That depends, lass. What did ye have in mind?"

After tossing the cloth aside, he prowled toward her.

"Well, if memory serves me correctly, we've coupled in four—no five—positions and we've been totally naked for each. I must admit I'm curious if it is possible to achieve satisfaction while partially clothed—"

With a growl, he was upon her, rucking her skirts to her waist, and freeing himself in a series of fluid motions. He entered her without preamble, and she smiled against his mouth. "I guess, that answers that question. I do have more, ye ken."

"God, Woman. Ye'll be the death of me," he rasped.

"Aye, but such a lovely way to die."

About the Author

USA Today Bestselling, award-winning author COLLETTE CAMERON® scribbles Scottish and Regency historicals featuring dashing rogues and scoundrels and the intrepid damsels who reform them.Blessed with an overactive and witty muse that won't stop whispering new romantic romps in her ear, she's lived in Oregon her entire life, though she dreams of living in Scotland part-time. A self-confessed Cadbury chocoholic, you'll always find a dash of inspiration and a pinch of humor in her sweet-to-spicy timeless romances®.

Explore **Collette's worlds** at
www.collettecameron.com!

Join her **VIP Reader Club** and **FREE newsletter**.
Giggles guaranteed!

FREE BOOK: Join Collette's The Regency Rose® VIP Reader Club to get updates on book releases, cover reveals, contests, and giveaways she reserves exclusively for email and newsletter followers. Also, any deals, sales, or special promotions are offered to club members first. She will not share your name or email, nor will she spam you.

http://bit.ly/TheRegencyRoseGift

Follow Collette on BookBub
https://www.bookbub.com/authors/collette-cameron

Other Collette Cameron Books

Heart of a Scot

To Love a Highland Laird

To Redeem a Highland Rogue

To Seduce a Highland Scoundrel

To Woo a Highland Warrior

To Enchant a Highland Earl

To Defy a Highland Duke

To Marry a Highland Marauder

To Bargain with a Highland Buccaneer

A Christmas Kiss for the Highlander

Check out Collette's Other Series

Castle Brides

Daughters of Desire

Seductive Scoundrels

The Culpepper Misses

The Honorable Rogues®

Chronicles of the Westbrook Brides

Highland Heather Romancing a Scot

Collections

Lords in Love

Heart of a Scot Books 1-3

The Honorable Rogues® Books 1-3

The Honorable Rogues® Books 4-6

Seductive Scoundrels Series Books 1-3

Seductive Scoundrels Series Books 4-6

The Culpepper Misses Series Books 1-2

~Coming Soon~

Daughters of Desire (Scandalous Ladies) Series Books 1-2

Highland Heather Romancing a Scot Series Books 1-2

From the Desk of Collette Cameron

One of the things I enjoy the most about writing historical romances is the research I do. I strive for historical accuracy, even though my writing is a mixture of fictitious and authentic places and people. I diligently try to present my stories within the cultural strictures of the period they are written in. However, I do not impose today's values or norms within my writing. For doing so not only detracts from my stories' authenticity, I believe it a disservice to the people who lived during that time and were obliged to live under much different and harsher expectations.

Toward that end, I would like to clarify a couple of points in TO SEDUCE A HIGHLAND SCOUNDREL.

King George I was a highly unpopular king. From the House of Hanover, he came to the throne at fifty-four years of age and ruled thirteen short years. Nowhere in my research was there any mention of him being a particularly religious or moral king. In fact, he is often suspected of having had his wife's lover murdered. However, I've taken artistic license in having him render harsh judgment on the people listed in the "journal" Berget refers to. Buggery (sodomy) was a felony and capital offense until 1861. That extended to pedophilia, though that particular term was not used during the 1700s.

Another factor that requires clarification is the reason Nairna spent her childhood in a French convent rather than in Scotland. Penal Laws implemented in the 1500s sought to restrict the Catholic faith in Scotland. These laws were in effect during Nairna's childhood, and though Scotland had many abbeys and priories, some of which still stand today, most were dissolved or secularized in the 1500s and 1600s.

Finally, though I did mention the Jacobite Risings in this book, because they weren't an integral part of the tale and the story was set between the two major uprisings, I didn't elaborate on them.

I thank you for reading TO SEDUCE A HIGHLAND SCOUNDREL, and I hope you enjoyed Graeme and Berget's tale. If you did, please consider leaving a review. I would be so grateful.

Hugs,

Collette

Connect with Collette!

Check out her author world:
collettecameron.com
Join her Reader Group:
www.facebook.com/groups/CollettesCheris
Subscribe to her newsletter, receive a FREE Book:
www.signup.collettecameron.com/TheRegencyRoseGift

To Woo a Highland Warrior

Heart of a Scot, Book Four

***He meant to rescue her.
He never thought she'd end up saving him...***

Baron Liam Mackay lost everything he ever loved. Now, he protects his heart behind a carefully constructed wall of indifference, refusing to actually *feel* anything. He'll focus instead on making sure his feudal barony is prosperous and simply avoid all marriage-minded women. Then he saves a lovely temptress from certain death, and all his well-laid plans completely fall apart...

Hired assassins don't target illegitimate orphans. Or so Emeline LeClaire *thought*, until it happened to her. But when a handsome Highlander steps in to save her, she can't help but feel that perhaps fate brought them together. Perhaps she can help save his wounded heart and soul just as he saved her life...

When a flash flood strands them together, can Emeline convince Liam to trust in love...and in her? Or will they remain star-crossed forever?

Printed in Great Britain
by Amazon